PRAYERS
of a
STRANGER
A Christmas Journey

ALSO BY DAVIS BUNN

Full Circle
Heartland
My Soul to Keep

❧

International Thrillers
Imposter
The Lazarus Trap
Elixir

❧

Novellas
The Book of Hours
Tidings of Comfort and Joy
One Shenandoah Winter

❧

For a complete listing of novels by Davis Bunn,
visit his website at davisbunn.com

PRAYERS
of a
STRANGER
A Christmas Journey

DAVIS BUNN

THOMAS NELSON
Since 1798

NASHVILLE DALLAS MEXICO CITY RIO DE JANEIRO

Published in Nashville, Tennessee, by Thomas Nelson. Thomas Nelson is a registered trademark of Thomas Nelson, Inc.

Thomas Nelson, Inc., books may be purchased in bulk for educational, business, fund-raising, or sales promotional use. For information, please e-mail SpecialMarkets@ ThomasNelson.com.

Scriptures taken from the HOLY BIBLE, NEW INTERNATIONAL VERSION®, NIV®. Copyright © 1973, 1978, 1984, 2011 by Biblica, Inc.™ Used by permission of Zondervan. All rights reserved worldwide. www.zondervan.com.

Publisher's Note: This novel is a work of fiction. Names, characters, places, and incidents are either products of the author's imagination or used fictitiously. All characters are fictional, and any similarity to people living or dead is purely coincidental.

Library of Congress Cataloging-in-Publication Data

Bunn, T. Davis, 1952-
  Prayers of a stranger : a Christmas journey / Davis Bunn.
    p. cm.
  ISBN 978-0-8499-4488-8 (trade paper : alk. paper)
1. Christmas stories. I. Title.
  PS3552.U4718P69 2012
  813'.54--dc23

           2012020559

Printed in the United States of America
12 13 14 15 16 QG 5 4 3 2 1

This book is dedicated to Ami McConnell, whose unique vision has helped shape my story. Thank you, friend.

CHAPTER ONE

Amanda entered the hospital through the crash doors. They were named such partly because they opened into the reception area serving the accident and emergency wards and intensive care. But it was mostly because of the sound the ambulances made when they swooped in and pulled out the gurneys and came rushing inside. Florida summer deluges could dump as much as a foot of rain in a few hours, storms so intense they exploded off the pavement and splattered a fine mist out fifty feet. The winds that sometimes came with these storms, particularly during hurricane season, made standard ER entrances impossible here. So the architects had wisely built a recessed entrance, with the hospital's other seven floors extending over the entire circular ER drive. No matter how violent the tempest, people could disembark in safety and remain dry. The shelter came at a cost, though; namely, sunlight. The gloom was legendary.

When she was appointed personal assistant to the hospital's director, Amanda's first act had been to rework the cave's lighting and institute free valet parking. She called them volunteers, but the parking attendants were all paid minimum wage. The free parking signs stated in bold letters that tipping was forbidden.

A large number of patients and visitors were elderly. This was, after all, Florida. They should not need to walk from the parking garage. Amanda's volunteers, many of them as old as the visitors, made for a cheerful counterpart to the cave's oppressive nature. They greeted newcomers with a smile and the promise that the care they found inside would be the best available anywhere. And because of their genial welcome, most people believed them. Or at least they entered a little less frightened than before.

The brightest light in the shadowy enclave came from the new miniature Christmas tree Amanda had put up the day before. Like so much else about Christmas in Florida, the effect was a bit jarring, but Amanda thought it was a nice touch nonetheless. Such actions came naturally to her. Others called it her gift, doing the things that made everyone feel better, staff and patients alike. She heard that time after time. The only trouble was, Amanda had no real interest in her present job. This had been true from the very first day. She had taken it as a means to escape. Nothing more.

Frank, her favorite of the parking attendants and her next-door neighbor, was on duty when she arrived. When his only sister, who'd never married, became critically ill, Frank and his wife, Emily, had moved down to see her through her final days. They had never left. Frank's sister had been in and out of the hospital for nine very hard months. Parking cars and greeting newcomers was Frank's way of saying thanks. His smile was constant, his heart as big as the Florida sky.

"If I didn't know better, I'd say there was going to be a coup today," he said.

"Not a chance," Amanda assured him. "I would have seen the memo."

"And I'm telling you, something more than the standard muttering is happening."

Amanda stepped away from the doors and waited while Frank helped an older woman unfold her walker and passed the car keys to another attendant. He announced with a grin, "Dr. Henri is smiling."

"Is this a joke?"

"Nope. Forehead to shirt collar. And about two hundred teeth."

"If I didn't know you, I'd say you had finally gone over the edge."

Dr. Henri was head of the emergency room staff. He was a wrinkled prune from the Dominican Republic and the finest ER doctor Amanda had ever met. He hated the American way of saying his first name, but if the French *Henri* was beyond the reach of many staffers, he loathed listening to them butcher his last name, which was Beausejour.

"I always assumed his frown was tattooed into place."

"The nurses all look stunned," Frank agreed. "This could only mean one thing, right? Moira has kicked the bucket."

"Not possible," Amanda replied and turned to leave. "I've gotten five e-mails from her already this morning."

❧

Amanda decided to go inspect this alleged smile for herself.

She was about to ask the nurse on station if the rumors were true when the impossible happened. Through the open doorway leading to the ready room, Amanda heard humming.

The nurse said softly, "If I'm dreaming, don't pinch me. I never want to wake up."

Amanda asked, "He's in there?"

"None other. Amazing, huh?"

"What's happened?"

"I've been afraid to ask."

The doctor emerged from the ready room and smiled. "If it isn't my favorite lady. How are you, Amanda?"

She shared round eyes with the nurse. "Fine, Dr. Henri."

"Walk with me, please."

All but one of the treatment stations were empty, as was customary for that time of day. Dr. Henri briefly checked the status of his lone patient as they passed, then said, "Your neighbor Frank is leaving us."

"What?"

"He's been having pains in his hips. You've probably noticed the way he rocks when he walks. He has serious deterioration of both joints."

"He told me it was arthritis."

"That's what he's told everyone. Including his wife. He wanted to keep it quiet, but I thought you should know."

"I certainly should."

"Frank doesn't want any fuss. He says the best way for him to leave is assuming he will soon return."

Amanda nodded her understanding. Frank was facing an

ordeal of six months, perhaps longer. Surgery, rehab, then the second round on the other hip.

Dr. Henri stopped by the elevator. "He's due to have his first operation in January."

"Did you know Frank and Emily are supposed to leave for Israel next week? Frank says she's been dreaming of this trip for years."

"He told me. He doesn't want to go. It would be good if you could help break the news to Emily. If Frank goes, he'll need to use either a walker or perhaps even a wheelchair."

"Which he would positively loathe."

"Traveling would be painful. And he could well face the risk of further deterioration in a foreign land."

"I'll handle it," Amanda promised.

"Yes, that is what you are best at. Handling things."

When Dr. Henri started to turn away, Amanda stopped him. "I was looking for you to find out what's going on today. Why are you smiling?"

Dr. Henri's beaming face was awesome to behold. "Why, Amanda Vance. Shame on you. Doctors don't deal in rumors. We're trained to remain above all that."

✑

Amanda had insisted on taking the least appealing office as her own. It was little more than a walk-in closet, long and narrow and angled like a crooked elbow. Her lone window was up too high to grant her a view of anything save the sky. During her early days on the job she had sat at her empty desk and watched the square of light crawl across the wall opposite her desk. She'd needed a position inside the hospital that would take her away from nursing and grant her space to heal. But within a few weeks she had found her job becoming as high-stressed as anything she had known.

But she had also found a new home.

Amanda stopped by the desk of Harriet, the secretary she shared with four other administrators. "Anything?"

"The witch has called for you. Five times."

Hardly a surprise. Amanda asked, "Anything important?"

Harriet was a hard-bitten lifer whose laugh was a single bounce of her shoulders. "Cute."

Amanda heard her phone ringing and hurried into her cubbyhole. "This is Amanda."

It was the ER nurse on the line. "Did Dr. Henri tell you what has him doing a jig?"

"Dr. Henri is dancing now?"

"Close enough. What did he say?"

"Nothing. Not a peep."

"Did you ask?"

"Of course I did. He just smiled." Amanda changed the subject. "Did you hear that Frank is leaving?"

"Yes. And he wants us to just let him slip away without any fuss at the end of the day."

"Are we going to let him?"

"When did we ever listen to what men want?"

Amanda hung up the phone, stowed her smile away, and told Harriet, "I'm going upstairs."

The woman gave her a jaded smile. "Better you than me."

༺ঌ༻

When the elevator doors opened on the seventh floor, Amanda knew something had happened. Nurses learned to notice small shifts in their ward's atmosphere. This sixth sense might be scoffed at by outsiders, but Amanda had no doubt that her ability to detect subtle signs had saved a number of lives. This morning her antennae were twitching.

She had not really wanted the job of administrative assistant to the hospital director. But Dr. Henri, one of the hospital's three senior doctors, had insisted it was this or go back to being a floor nurse. Which she couldn't. Not then. Perhaps not ever.

Amanda had been looking for a quiet corner where she could regroup following what she silently referred to as her Christmas ordeal. Which had actually happened the week after Thanksgiving the year before. But Dr. Henri had been adamant. The doctors knew Amanda and they trusted her. Which was more than any of them could say for the hospital's new director, Moira Campbell.

Moira had turned the hospital against her on the very first day. Amanda had been out on maternity leave, so she missed the worst of it. Apparently the new director had turned up her nose at the former director's office and demanded the one used by his predecessor. The fact that it had been redone as the doctors' lounge meant nothing to her. The doctors were evicted, Moira instated, and the battle was on.

The throne room, as it was now known, occupied the southeast corner of the hospital's top floor. Three wings intersected there, one housing the new heart center, the second radiology, and the third, a stubby afterthought, contained the hospital's legal and Medicare staff. Moira Campbell's office stood at the end of a long lonely corridor, from where she ruled her fiefdom in isolated splendor.

Amanda had insisted upon remaining downstairs, and the doctors had backed her. Her primary duty was liaison with the hospital staff, they had told Moira, and this role would best be handled from the hospital's nerve center. In truth it had worked out best for them both. Amanda could take Moira in small doses. So long as she was not forced to remain in the woman's company for too long, she managed to treat Moira with the same patience she did a squalling infant—check vitals, see if anything was needed, and if the baby just wanted to bawl, let her. And Moira was most comfortable with her computer and her balance sheets. It was people she couldn't handle.

Amanda knocked on the closed door. "You wanted to see—"

Moira did not pause in the process of dumping the contents of a drawer into a cardboard box. "I'm being reassigned."

A trio of thoughts flashed through Amanda's mind. First, Dr. Henri did indeed have a valid reason for smiling. Second, Amanda would soon be experiencing considerable pleasure as official deliverer of this news. And third, heaven help any patient who arrived in dire need of care today.

Moira demanded, "Don't you have anything to say?"

Amanda shrugged, a gesture she despised seeing in one of the sullen young trainees. But she couldn't say what she was thinking. It would be like pouring oil on an open flame. Finally she settled on, "Who is your replacement?"

"Oh, I don't know. Someone from HQ."

The hospital's owners were based in Boston. Which was

where Moira had come from. The prospect of another Moira clone dampened Amanda's joy. A little.

Moira Campbell had probably once been quite attractive. But something had happened along the way, and Amanda suspected it had to do with a man. Now Moira was a parody of herself. Her pale blue eyes had grown flat and guarded. She wore too-flashy clothes; her hair was kept to a pageboy cut that did not suit her at all, and its orange DayGlo color could only have come from a bottle. Her pinched face and suspicious air invited people to dislike her.

Amanda turned to the window and stifled the urge to break into song. The view from Moira's office was stupendous, out over rooftops to the inland waterway. The barrier island was a brilliant green ribbon in the distance. Amanda asked, "When is your replacement arriving?"

"Tomorrow." Moira upended another drawer into her box. "I've been ordered to vacate the premises before the new boy arrives. No official transfer. Nothing. It's a scandal."

"Can I give you a hand packing?"

"No, thank you very much. You're no doubt delighted to see the back of me."

Amanda caught herself in the act of nodding agreement. Beyond the window a sailboat cut through the inland waterway. She wondered what it would be like to spend days in such a carefree manner, separated from the world and its many woes, free to go where the wind took her.

Moira hammered a stack of files into an already full box. "You have a special place in my end-of-duty report, I can promise you that."

Amanda decided she'd had enough. She stepped out of the

office, softly shut the door, and released a breath she had been holding for eleven months.

◦◦◦

The oddest thought struck her as she stepped into the elevator. Almost as though it had been waiting there for her to arrive.

Amanda's finger hovered over the third-floor button. Suddenly the elevator jerked and started down, as though it had grown tired of waiting for her to make up her mind.

Amanda pressed the button.

The ob-gyn and infant care departments had a guard station directly opposite the elevators. One could not be too careful with babies these days. No one was permitted on the floor without an appointment. Everyone was checked in.

The duty nurse was a new face, young and alert. Amanda did not recognize her, which was hardly a surprise, since she had not been on the ward for almost a year. The nurse checked her admin ID, asked her to sign the registry, and smiled her through.

It was all familiar, and so very alien. Her former boss, Dr. Frost, had retired two weeks after Amanda's departure. She of course knew the ward's new senior doctor, but spoke with him only when it could not be avoided. She assumed he had heard of her breakdown, for the new doctor treated her with the sort of gentle patience awarded the most frightened mothers.

Amanda did a quick tour of her former world, past the birth stations, the patient ward, their own radiology room, which she had fought so hard to install. She continued down the hall outside the newborns' chambers and did not stop until she arrived at the critical care unit. The glass wall overlooked the nine incubators, three of which held premies. This was where she had most belonged. Her world.

A nurse she recognized despite the mask and blue hairnet walked over, checked the infant's vitals, wrote them into the chart, then noticed Amanda. Her eyes widened. She waved tentatively. Amanda wanted to respond. But her hand was too heavy to lift, and a smile would have been a lie. She stood like that at the entrance to the unit, filled with longing and regret, then turned and walked away.

As the elevator doors closed, Amanda whispered to herself, "One day."

If only she could convince herself the words were true.

CHAPTER TWO

B y the time she arrived back downstairs, news of
Moira Campbell's departure was all over the hospital.
Laughter and light chatter filled the hallway, sounds
from the hour before a party started. As she opened the doors
leading to the admin wing, she saw two nurses hug and a pair of
interns exchange a high five. Oh, yes. They'd heard.

The battle-scarred Harriet, whose favorite pastime was
counting down to retirement, greeted her with, "Tell me you're
not leaving too."

"Excuse me?"

"Don't think for an instant your work is done here."

To her astonishment several worried faces emerged from
neighboring cubicles. She realized what was going on. "You
can't possibly have heard about my stopping by the infant
ward."

"Oh, please. CNN has nothing on this place for spreading
news."

The senior bookkeeper slipped from her office. "So it's true, you're leaving?"

Harriet demanded, "Who's supposed to pave the way for us with the new suit?"

"Who says you'll be needing anyone?" Amanda countered.

She sniffed her disdain. "He's coming from the home office, isn't that right?"

"How could you possibly know this?"

"It's how we survive down here in the burrows."

"All right. Yes. Boston is sending someone from HQ."

"So now we get Moira Two."

"For all you know he could be a perfect prince. Don't look at me—" Amanda stopped because Dr. Henri had stepped through the doorway. "Yes?"

"I'd like another word, Amanda."

"Tell her she's got to stay," her secretary said. "Tie her to her desk. Give me a call if you need a hand."

Dr. Henri moved to the door to her office and waited. "Now, please."

᠅

Dr. Henri settled into the chair opposite her desk and studied the whiteboards lining her side wall. Light from the narrow window shone off the screws clamping the boards in place. "The orderliness of your thinking never ceases to amaze me."

The boards had been segmented into all the operations within the administrative process. Every incomplete task was visible, along with due dates and related problems. When Moira or a department director requested an update, all Amanda needed to do was step to her side wall. It was similar to the status board used with high-risk infants; that was updated hourly and showed each new shift the precise status of each child. The other admin personnel considered Amanda's invention a marvel. Except for Moira, of course. She had never entered Amanda's office. "Thanks."

"Amanda, do you really want to return to nursing?"

"Why is this anyone else's business?"

"Answer the question, please."

"I don't know what I want." Amanda knew she sounded shrill. "Until last year all I ever hoped to do with my life was care for babies."

He gestured toward the hallway. "That wasn't an act. The admin staff is terrified of losing you."

"But *why?*"

"Because you care. Your first thought is for the hospital staff. You stand up to the director, to the doctors, to the board, to Boston. For them. Do you know what they call you out there? Vice President of Calming the Waters."

Amanda was speechless. Because she had always considered this a temporary position, she had never even requested a job description, much less a title. "I don't . . . I was just doing my job."

"Yes, you were. And quite splendidly. If it is your aim to return to nursing, I will help you. But at the moment I can only add my voice to theirs. Stay. Help us all through the transition."

"I may not have any choice." Amanda related her final exchange with Moira.

Dr. Henri had the remarkable ability to frown with his entire being. "Her final report will bias the new director against you. Was that why you returned by way of the infant station?"

"No, well, it wasn't . . ." She sighed. "I don't know why I went. I couldn't even push open the door."

He showed no surprise. "You're a nurse. You know there is a cycle of healing, and you know it takes longer than anyone wishes. Especially wounds to the heart."

"Can I really? Heal?"

"You *are* healing. You *will* be whole again."

There was no reason why words spoken by the doctor who most frightened the hospital's nurses should cause her eyes to tear up. "I wish I could believe you."

"I suggest you go away. Take a vacation. You have time coming, don't you?"

"Three weeks."

"Use it. Give the incoming director a chance to hear from the rest of us just how vital you are."

This time she found it necessary to wipe her eyes. "We can't. Chris's company is downsizing. He's under so much pressure right now . . ."

She stopped talking because Dr. Henri had risen to his feet. "In fact, I suggest you leave today."

◆

All the news raced ahead of Amanda throughout the day: Moira's departure, Frank's pending operation, Amanda's visit to the baby ward, Amanda's pending time off. Hospital staff she had never spoken to stopped to ask what she was going to do with her holiday and tell her how much they would miss having her around. She decided to stop by the gift shop on her way out and buy Frank a card. And then, while he was held captive at the party he had tried to avoid—as if they would ever let their Frank go without a fuss—she would have the chat with his wife that Dr. Henri had requested.

With less than four weeks to go, Christmas dominated the shop. Carols played through overhead speakers. Displays wished everyone the season's cheer. Until eleven months ago it had been one of her favorite times of year.

Amanda slipped past an older woman inspecting the plush toys and stopped in front of the cards. With an abrupt shudder her world seized up.

There before her were row after row of baby cards. Congratulating the family. Glittering with happy best wishes. Amanda's chest became so constricted she could not breathe.

She wrenched herself around as though she were yanking herself free of a nightmare.

But the opposite side of the aisle held something even worse.

She now faced row after row of birthday cards. And directly in front of her was a sparkling card wishing every joy on the baby's first birthday.

She was outside the shop gasping for breath before she realized she had heard someone call her name. She forced her legs to carry her out and away.

CHAPTER THREE

C ell phone in hand, Chris Vance paced back and forth in front of his office window, thinking about how much he wanted to hit the road. He was born with a greyhound's love of open spaces. When he ran, he was not only free, he was in his element.

Everyone knew he ran at midday. Including Claire, his sister, who seemed to take an oddly possessive pleasure at holding him up. The middle child of five, Claire seemed to consider it her role in life to bind the family together.

"This year Christmas is going to be *super*," she declared. "Tony's sister is *finally* coming. I've only been begging her for *six* years. Did I tell you she's pregnant with number three?"

"No, Claire. You didn't." Which was hardly a surprise, since Chris had not seen his brother-in-law's siblings since Claire's wedding. Claire's husband, Tony, was a genial man, an orthodontist who could calm the most frightened child, even when they faced years of braces.

Chris tried to stifle a blade of envy. Claire's family would never face the risk of losing their jobs and their home. The world would always produce more kids with bad teeth.

"Dad is coming, of course. And Pete with their two, and Samantha with her brood. And Sally. That makes, let's see . . . nineteen plus you two, twenty-one! Isn't that *fabulous*?"

"Claire, I don't think we'll be able to make it this year."

"But you *have* to. We *always* have Christmas together. It's the best time of the year!"

"Not . . . Sorry."

"Doesn't Amanda know how *important* this is?"

"We haven't discussed it."

"I'll call her. She *has* to let you—"

"Don't you do any such thing." His tone hardened. "If you push her, she'll agree. And I don't want that."

"But *why*?"

"Do you even remember what happened last Christmas?"

"Chris. That was *months* ago. You've got to get over it."

"Claire, if one of your children died, do you think you'd be 'over it' in a year?"

There was a gasp, then, "It's not the same thing at all!"

"It feels that way to Amanda."

"Well, she's wrong. Chris, I want you here! With us! Where you *belong*!"

This was the other side of Claire that few people saw, mostly because they knew it was easier to let her enthusiasm sweep them along. Chris was one of the few people who didn't instantly jump on Claire's bandwagon. He did not argue; he simply did not budge. It was one of the reasons why he was happy to be living in Florida instead of nearer to the rest of the brood. He loved Claire. But his sister could be a bully.

"You need to understand—"

"I understand *perfectly*. I called you about *Christmas*. And you two are going to *ruin* it." Claire slammed down the phone.

Chris stood there a long moment, staring blindly out his window. For once the sunlight did not beckon. It was not the conversation that anchored him to his desk. His sister Claire was insensitive, but that wasn't the problem. Chris felt the silence echo with the thousands of prayers he had uttered over the past eleven months. More than anything he yearned for his wife to come back to life.

Then he left the office and went for a run.

෴

Brevard County was a blue-collar sort of place. Cape Canaveral and Cape Kennedy had seen to that. Even the more expensive neighborhoods were dominated by folks who did physical labor for a living. One county farther south, Indian River, everything changed. The Sebastian Inlet Bridge connected the two barrier islands, but the world down there was a different place entirely. The island community of Vero Beach was home to some of the richest people on earth. They owned three-million-dollar oceanfront condos, parked Bentley convertibles in their garages, and only used the places for the season, which ran from the week after New Year's to the week before Easter.

Amanda always insisted on Chris driving her down for dinner once each season. She treated it like a visit to the zoo. As she pulled into her drive, she realized that they had not made the trip last year. Like so much else it had been forgotten in the frantic struggle to push the December events away.

Chris was not home, which was hardly a surprise. Before the economic meltdown they normally tried to time their arrivals so they could have dinner together. But with his company struggling to survive, his hours had become crazy. She glanced across the road to the Wrights' drive. She'd get that errand over with before entering her empty house.

They lived in a cul de sac in Melbourne Beach, the county's most residential beachside community. The town had no hotel and only three oceanfront condos. The beaches were all public, yet held a locals-only atmosphere. Mothers camped there on pretty days and shared baby-minding with their neighbors. Kids who misbehaved found themselves catching it from everywhere.

The atmosphere even carried over into the water. Local Melbourne Beach surfers made newcomers welcome and helped newbies learn the ropes. Twenty miles farther south, Sebastian Inlet was home to the largest waves on the Eastern Seaboard. There the vibe was totally different, fueled by outsiders hunting the limelight and a place on the professional circuit.

Melbourne Beach had managed to remain like the place where Amanda had grown up—Cocoa Beach, which over the years had become steadily more crowded and frenetic. Her father was retired NASA, her mom a schoolteacher. All she ever wanted was to put down her roots in Brevard County and raise a happy brood of six or seven kids. But with the economic downturn, Chris's work situation was uncertain. And their plans for a family were on hold. Maybe forever. Amanda crossed the street and wished for a way to turn the page. Start over. Build the life she and Chris had dreamed of.

Their neighbors Frank and Emily lived in a Florida-style

home whose stucco finish and wood-slat blinds made it almost a twin of their own. But this time of year, the difference between the two households could not have been more startling. The Wrights' front lawn contained two mock Christmas trees, the house was rimmed by lights, and every sunset twelve deer frolicked in electronic abandon. Amanda had kept her front curtains shut since Thanksgiving, waiting for the holiday season to be over and done.

Emily opened the door and gaped. "It's you!"

"What's the matter?"

"Look here. What's this in my hand?"

Amanda glanced at the phone. "Is this a trick question?"

Emily pulled her inside and shut the door. "I picked this up to call you, and here you are! It's a miracle."

"No, it's not."

"How do you know?"

"If God had a miracle in mind, he'd choose someone better than me to deliver it."

"Oh, piffle." Emily led her into the kitchen. A red enamel pot sat on the stove and filled the kitchen with a rich aroma. "Have you eaten?"

"Not since breakfast," Amanda said. "Things got out of hand at the hospital today."

"I'm not surprised, given what I've heard. Sit there at the counter. We can talk while you eat." She used a potholder to lift the top. "I'm making veal *pot au feau*, which is fancy French for beef stew. It's Frank's favorite, and it was ready an hour ago."

As Emily filled a flat bowl with a generous helping of flaky veal and potatoes and leeks and carrots, Amanda studied her neighbor. Emily was in her early sixties, a rotund woman with a face made to smile. They had bought this house just before

Thanksgiving a year ago. During that time, Amanda had become an expert at keeping life and people at arm's length. She knew the Wrights had four children and thought they all lived up north, but she did not even know their names. "Why aren't you at Frank's farewell party?"

"What is there to celebrate? And from the sound of things, I'll be over at the hospital plenty in the weeks ahead."

"Then you know about his hip?"

"Of course I know. I see him limping around. I knew it couldn't possibly be arthritis. I had a long talk with our GP, who was informed by the gentleman doctor at the hospital with the interesting name."

Amanda took a bite and declared, "This is fabulous."

"My parents started a family-style bistro in Chicago. I spent my teenage years waiting tables and learning to love good food."

"I never knew that."

"Hardly a surprise, given what you've been through."

The comment was said in an easy, matter-of-fact way. Amanda set her fork on the side of the plate and tried to clear away the sudden knot in her throat.

"What's the matter?"

"Nothing. It's just . . . you're so understanding. I'm afraid Chris's family will be expecting us for Christmas, and I'm just not ready for that."

Emily stood on the counter's other side, the ladle forgotten in her hand. "What about your folks?"

"They've learned not to talk about it. But I know what they're thinking. They want me to let go and heal." Amanda stirred the remnants of stew in her bowl. "If only it were that easy."

"You know what they say, dear. God gave us friends to make

up for our families." Emily pulled over a stool. "But can we save that discussion for later? There's something I wanted to ask you before Frank gets home."

Amanda gave her a questioning look.

"Frank can't go to Israel, of course. But the trip is booked and paid for. If we back out, we'll lose almost everything we've paid. And I certainly don't want to go by myself. So why don't you come with me?"

"Excuse me?"

"To Israel. Instead of Frank. Do you have a passport?"

"Sure. But I can't go."

"Why not?"

"I can't imagine what Chris would think about this. Especially now."

"Your husband is one of the most capable people I've ever met. He'll be fine, and you know it. My guess is he'll say this is a great idea. A miracle. You wait and see."

This time there was a soft resonance to the word *miracle*. Like a subtle push of unseen wind. "But why me? You've got family. Daughters. What about—"

"I've called. I've begged. They're all busy with Christmas. More stew?"

"What? No. Thank you."

"I was at the end of my rope, I can tell you. Then I thought about you. I know that sounds like you're my fall-back position."

"Sort of. A little."

"But when the idea came to me, it seemed like a gift." Emily's eyes shone. "I've seen you struggle this entire year, doing your absolute best to make yourself whole again. I know what you're going through. You *deserve* this."

Once again a lump became lodged in Amanda's throat, making her words sound strangled. "How could you possibly know what I've been going through?"

Emily's movements became very deliberate. She rinsed Amanda's bowl and wiped the counter and folded the towel and patted it down. "Come with me."

Emily led her back through the living room and down the hall and through a pair of double doors. The master bedroom was fronted by a small room, like a second foyer, with just enough space for a television and a sofa and a pair of bookshelves and a reading lamp. "Frank calls this his sanity room. When the grandchildren come and their noise gets to him, he retreats in here." Emily pointed to the photographs on the back wall. "This is what I wanted to show you."

There were five pictures, four of them encircling one in the middle. Amanda knew Emily and Frank had four kids. She also knew what she was seeing.

"Her name was Rachel. She was my second baby."

The child in the central photo was not right. Amanda had heard the words often enough. It was a tragic litany that anyone who worked in the baby ward was forced to endure from time to time. No amount of sonograms and prenatal testing could prepare either the patients or the doctors.

The baby's face was improperly shaped. The eyes were dull, probably blind. Amanda found herself entering her nurse's mode, seeing with nine years' experience in infant care. She could name four life-threatening conditions on display in that photograph.

Emily traced one finger along the border of that little face. "She lived three days."

"I'm so sorry, Emily."

The older woman turned slowly, taking the time to stow away all the emotions, able to show Amanda a very real smile. "You are going to be just fine."

Amanda felt her eyes flood with tears. "I've been so afraid to hope."

"I know. All too well. But you will. It's already happening. You've done far better with your year of grief than I did, let me tell you. The only way I survived was having a three-year-old who needed me. How you've managed with no child at all, well, all I can say is, I've seldom met a stronger lady."

"Why didn't you tell me?"

"What's there to tell? That sometimes I still wake up in the middle of the night and hear my husband crying in his sleep, and know he's mourning a child who's been in heaven for twenty-eight years? That sometimes I stand at my rear window and see this sweet child playing in the pool? You were doing fine. You needed one person who didn't push you or console you or tell you a thing more than good morning. I've been praying for you for a year now, and my prayers have been answered."

Amanda did not know what to say. She did not even trust herself to return Emily's fierce embrace for fear of breaking down entirely.

"Enough of this," Emily said, releasing her and wiping her eyes. "Go tell Chris. And start packing. We leave in eight days."

CHAPTER FOUR

C hris did not even give Amanda a chance to finish. "I think you should go."

Amanda felt in a slight daze. The entire day had been one great swirl of events, pushing her forward whether she wanted to or not. "Will you even let me tell you the rest?"

"I imagine we'll be talking about this until you board the plane. But sure, go ahead. Tell me whatever you like."

"So it's all settled then?"

"This sounds like a perfect opportunity to me. I actually wondered if you should offer to go when Frank told me about his hip."

"When was this?"

"I don't know. Four, five days back. Is there any more of Emily's stew?"

She carried Chris's bowl back into the kitchen. "Did it even cross your mind to tell me about Frank?"

"Yes, Amanda. Of course it did." He watched her deposit the second helping in front of him. "This is great."

"Why didn't you say something?"

"Frank asked me to keep it quiet. The only reason he told me was I saw him limping and wincing while he cut his grass, and finished the yard for him."

"Why do you suppose he didn't want me to know?"

"He said he didn't want a fuss at the hospital."

"Well, he got one anyway. He's still trapped at their not-so-surprise party."

"He dreaded telling Emily. He figured they'd have an awful row. He was determined for her to go and equally set against going himself. He'll be relieved to know you're taking his place." Chris pushed his plate to one side and breathed happily. "That's it. One more bite and I'll explode."

"Then I suppose I'm really going," Amanda said, and wondered at the sudden flutter of fear. It wasn't the trip. She was honest enough to know that. It was the future. She'd spent a year focusing down tight as possible on just making it through each day. The idea of having something to actually look forward to left her feeling weightless.

Chris read her expression. "Aren't you even a little bit excited?"

"Of course," she replied quietly. "I'm thrilled."

Eight days.

❧

November and December were the finest months of Florida's calendar. The weather was clear and cool and very dry. Amanda saw things she had spent a year ignoring. Flocks of birds were arriving from the north, bringing with them a rainbow of songs that filled the gardens and parks. The sweltering hurricane season was gone, and the tourist hordes had not yet arrived. People crooned their hellos. They had time for their neighbors and for a good laugh. The days were good, the sunsets magnificent. The parks were filled with families. Even the angriest dog lost its ability to growl.

Christmas was given a special welcome by Florida locals. Many imported traditions from other regions and countries. Families shared dishes and tales and rituals. Neighbors blocked off the streets with sawhorses, and block parties became raucous events. People involved in the tourist trade took a long friendly look at families and communities, because the high-season rush would begin the following weekend. For many this would be the last easy breath they drew until Easter.

The days leading up to their departure were both rushed and endless. Amanda regretted her decision and she could not wait to get away. One moment she was so excited she could not breathe, the next she lamented ever agreeing to this madness.

When she confessed as much to Emily, the older woman replied, "Oh, good. I thought I was the only one going crazy."

Frank's limp grew much worse, or so it seemed to Amanda. He did his best to hide any discomfort, clearly not wanting to trouble his wife. But twice Amanda heard a soft grunt as he pried himself out of a chair. When Emily was not around, he tended to swing with each step. Amanda realized he'd been hiding a great deal and told him as much four days before they departed. His only response was, "Don't let on."

At the hospital the new director's arrival was delayed, and delayed again. Dr. Henri and the other two senior doctors served as interim administrators. Harriet checked in with Amanda every day. The afternoon before their departure, she called four times in the space of an hour. Finally Amanda complained, "If I were in the office you wouldn't bother me with any of these things. If I'd even offered a suggestion you'd have bitten my head off."

"All right," Harriet relented. "This is positively the last time today."

"For the next twelve days," Amanda corrected. "You're not to call me."

"Don't talk crazy."

"I'm on vacation, Harriet."

"But the sky might fall!"

"It won't. And if it does, I'll be too far away to do anything about it." Amanda changed the subject. "Have you heard anything more about the new man?"

"Only that he's a monster."

"Oh, stop."

"But a handsome monster. And he's supposed to arrive the day after tomorrow. I'll call you the instant he shows up."

"Don't. I'll find out soon enough."

"But—"

"Good-bye, Harriet. Be nice to the new guy."

"Wait, wait. Dr. Henri wants a word. That's actually why I called."

Amanda sighed. "Put him on."

The ER chief sounded impossibly cheerful. "I've spoken with Trevor."

"Who?"

"Trevor Manning. Our new director."

"Harriet says he's supposed to be a monster."

Dr. Henri's laugh carried a rusty quality, as though it had

remained disused for far too long. "He seems nice enough to me. A bit nervous, which is hardly a surprise. I understand we're his first directorship."

"Is that good or bad?"

"I'll let you know when you return. He phoned to ask me my impressions of you."

Amanda felt her pulse quicken. "What did you tell him?"

"That Moira Campbell would have not survived as long as she did without you. He apparently didn't believe me, because he then called Dr. Frost."

Dr. Frost was Amanda's former boss, head of both the ob-gyn and maternity wards, an intensely intelligent and impatient man who lived up to his name. He still occasionally served as locum.

"And?"

"Dr. Frost said any hospital in the nation would be lucky to have you as senior nurse or admin chief. He also said the company should put you in as the new director."

"He didn't."

"There's more. Trevor called one of the other senior doctors who hadn't heard you were going on leave. The poor man apparently panicked on the phone. He told Trevor to expect seismic tremors and catastrophic events. Then Trevor made the mistake of mentioning Moira's comments. I'm wondering if Trevor's delayed arrival is due to blisters of the auditory canal."

Amanda didn't know what to say.

Dr. Henri must have found humor in her silence for he went on, "I spoke with the poor man again this morning. I assured him we in the ER were trained to remain calm in the face of multiple crises. We would lurch on without you. But I couldn't speak for the rest of the hospital." His chuckle lurked just below the surface. "Have a wonderful trip, Amanda. And when you return, I have one bit of advice."

"Yes?"

"Ask for a raise. A big one."

✦

"Is it too late to change my mind?" Chris asked.

They had decided they didn't want to share their last night before her departure with anyone else. So Chris had stoked the grill with mesquite coals and slow-roasted quail he'd brought home from his last hunting trip with his brother. Amanda dressed the backyard table with a linen tablecloth and her best china. When the slow-motion Florida sunset finally gave way to dusk, she lit a dozen candles and formed a glowing island. The palms became sentinels protecting their haven, and from the oleander hedge a mockingbird sang the most plaintive tune Amanda had ever heard. She replied, "It is, and you know it."

"I'll starve."

"You won't. You cook better than I do." She shifted her chair around so she could take hold of his hand. In the growing dusk, his face looked carved with eons of worry. "What's the matter?"

He shifted in his seat. "I have a meeting scheduled with a new client. A Brazilian company, Campaeo, that's moving into the area. I'm afraid it could be a disastrous connection for our group."

Amanda stared at her husband. Chris was so strong, so self-reliant, it was unsettling to see him so worried. And he never talked about his work at home. It was one of the things she had often found irritating, at least before last December. Since then she had been grateful not to have anything else to deal with. She knew Avery Electronics was going through a very hard time. She knew they might go under. She also knew Chris would do his utmost to save them. "Why do they bother you?"

"They have a terrible reputation. I've checked." He shifted again. "I'm sorry, I shouldn't have brought it up."

"I'm glad you did."

"Not the night before you leave. I apologize."

Amanda found herself needing to make a confession of her own. She took a very hard breath and said, "I feel as though I've been asleep for a year."

"I know exactly what you mean." His eyes glittered in the dwindling light. "I'm so sorry, Amanda."

"What on earth do you have to be sorry about?"

"I should have been there for you more than I was. You've been through so much."

The sunset's final remnants trembled and swam. "What about you, with everything you've had to go through at work."

"I shouldn't have let it bother me like I did."

"You love your job. And the company."

"That doesn't change anything."

"Of course it does. It's not like I was the only one who lost the baby. We both did."

"I know. But still."

The mockingbird called again, silencing them both. Amanda felt as though she was struggling to bring her husband into focus. As though she had not truly *looked* at him for twelve long months. She saw the new lines of stress that the burdens of this past year had etched deep. He was a gentle soul, with a voice to match. But his was a tensile strength. He could bend, but he would not break.

Amanda wished she could speak what was on her heart, but a blanket of uncertainty stifled her. What if all she felt was merely a fleeting desire born of her coming departure? What if she returned to discover that the easy love they had once known was truly gone forever?

Finally Chris rose and said, "You need to get some sleep."

Amanda followed her husband into the house. The unspoken words drifted in the night air, a lingering trace of conflicting emotions. *I want to wake up again.*

❦

Later that night Amanda woke from a dream she could not remember. She felt gripped by a terrible fear. Cold, half-formed thoughts wrapped around her throat and threatened to cut off her air. She rose from the bed and silently padded from the room.

Chris's words at sunset came back to her, along with the worry. He had seemed almost ancient as he spoke, a good man brought low by events beyond his control. With this fracture in the masculine wall he had built between work and home, she felt as though her world had tilted on its axis. The concern had unsettled even her dreams.

Her husband's Bible was open on the kitchen table. Two mornings each week, Chris led a men's study group at their church. He took the responsibility very seriously. She traced her finger along the text that was both highlighted and underlined. Her husband seemed very close to her then, as though he had risen from the bed to comfort her and read with her. She felt a swooping regret over leaving and flying off. Perhaps she should stay, call Emily first thing and . . .

A sudden memory flooded her, one she had not thought of in years. When she was seven, she had become caught in a riptide. She was an excellent swimmer and had heard the same lectures and warnings as every other Florida schoolchild. But nothing could have prepared her for the tide's invisible strength. The current clutched her and swept her out to sea. One moment she had been ten feet from the beach, the next moment the people standing and pointing her way were tiny bits of color on the distant shore.

Even though she was terrified, Amanda remembered the lessons. She did not fight. She lay on her back and swam parallel to the shore, gradually drawing herself out of the current's grip. She felt the instant the tide released her and she entered calmer waters. Soon as that happened, she turned so that she was now aimed back toward the shore. She remained on her back, because she knew if she turned over and looked to where her mother stood and shouted, she would panic. She'd start floundering just like the children in the film they had all been shown. So she remained on her back, doing as the instructors had said, swimming at a pace she could keep up for a long time. And she started singing to keep herself company. Over and over, one line from her favorite song, *Jesus loves me this I know*. It was a silly thing to do, singing the words while she paddled. But suddenly everything was just fine. And the calm stayed with her until the lifeguard arrived on his paddleboard and called her the bravest girl he'd ever met, and then said it again when they arrived back on the shore and her tear-streaked mother hugged her and Amanda finally gave in to the shakes.

That night she told her father that Jesus had met her in the water and stayed with her until the lifeguard came, so that she wouldn't be alone or afraid. And her father had gotten tears in his eyes and he said that he was sure she was right.

Amanda closed the Bible and fingered its worn leather cover. Then she rose and went back to bed. She spooned up against her husband and shut her eyes. She knew the trip was a good thing. Important. How she knew this was less important than the sensation that her going was vital.

She slept and did not dream.

CHAPTER FIVE

A n hour into the flight from Orlando to London, Amanda finally realized how exhausted the week's events had left her. The flight attendant had delivered them little glasses of ice and Coke, and the cabin filled with the fragrances of their coming meal. Then she was out like a light.

When she opened her eyes, Amanda had no idea how long she had slept. The hands on her watch meant nothing. Her tray had been lowered, and a meal was there waiting for her. Emily must have decided Amanda would like the pasta. The sauce was congealed, but she was famished and ate it anyway. The shades were down on the windows. A few people read, while others watched the entertainment screens. The flickering images formed little beacons in the gloom and the rushing sound.

Most of the passengers around her were asleep. As was Emily beside her. Amanda knew her neighbor was sixty-three and had always considered her young for her age, but in repose the strains of life were very clear on her face. Amanda wondered at the course of events that had brought Emily to this place.

She lifted her tray, slipped from the chair, and took her meal back to the galley. She visited the washroom, then returned to her seat. The noise and the dark formed a cocoon around her chair. She felt disconnected from the world and everything that she had left behind. Even the events of the previous year were somehow removed, as though she had finally found a way to put them at arm's length. The weight of regret was still with her, but lighter now.

Amanda pulled her small New Testament from her purse. She read, but was not held by the verses. She prayed, but the words formed a soft rush, like water passing through a stream that had neither beginning nor end. She shut her eyes and reveled in freedom at forty thousand feet. For the first time she found herself growing genuinely excited over what lay ahead, the ancient lands and the far dawn.

Nine hours against the wind to London. A two-hour layover in a cheerless Heathrow waiting room. Another five-hour flight to Israel. By the time they landed in Tel Aviv, Amanda felt disconnected and completely spent.

Emily staggered along beside her, leaning to her right as though her purse held bricks. They slipped into the line at customs, then passed into a circular chamber. The room was a work of art, a silent welcome to another world. The ceiling rose to a central opening through which poured both daylight and a waterfall. The pool at the base formed a circular enclave around which people sat and read and lounged.

Emily asked, "Am I dreaming?"

"If you are, I'm having the same dream."

"I feel as though I'm standing in David's cave."

Amanda found herself thinking of all the people she had read about, the families that had struggled for generations to escape and come to Israel. The sacrifices they had been forced to make. A thousand different languages, a million different tales of hardship and toil. And here was Israel's response: a jewel of a room that spoke what words could not ever say, a song as constant and timeless as the waterfall. Welcome home.

⌀

Their tour guide gathered them in stages and camped them by the airport café. Amanda was not hungry until she spied the breakfast pastries; then she ate two and shared a third with Emily. They were light as air and drizzled with a coating of honey and ground pistachios and diced apricots. Emily declared, "Every breakfast I ever have will be compared to this."

Finally their guide shepherded them out to the waiting bus. They rumbled swiftly through the flatlands and began grinding up into the Jerusalem hills. The tour guide had a nasal voice and a tone that suggested she knew no one was listening. But her job required her to speak just the same, so she described how the modern highway was laid upon Roman stones and followed the same course as David's army. She spoke of the more recent invaders and pointed out the rusting hulks of armored personnel carriers and tanks, remnants of the '47 uprising that led to the birth of the new Israel. Amanda tried to listen, but the words just spilled over her, especially when Jerusalem's ancient walls

41

came into view. A crown of golden stone rose on the hilltop, and suddenly the burden of fatigue was much easier to bear.

As they pulled into the hotel forecourt, the tour guide said, "You will all wait patiently in line while your names are read off by the receptionist. There will be no argument over room placement, please. Not everyone can have a view of the Old City."

As they filed obediently off the bus, Amanda realized that Emily's cheeks were wet. "Are you all right?"

"I'm better than that." Emily wiped her face. "I've dreamed of this all my life."

The guide's impatient voice was as insignificant as a buzzing fly. Amanda took her friend's hand and said, "I'm glad I came."

❧

The next four days were one constant blur, each full to bursting. Amanda felt so rushed her feet scarcely touched the ground. Day one, they took a walking tour of Jerusalem. Day two was the Mount of Olives and the Valley of the Tombs and the highlands and the Roman coliseum. Day three was the Valley of Armageddon and Nazareth and Caesarea. Day four was the Sea of Galilee, Tiberius, Capernaum, and the Golan Heights.

By the time they arrived back at the hotel each evening, Amanda was scarcely able to keep her eyes open through dinner. Her nightly conversations with Chris were a swift good night, a soft whisper of love that she needed but was too exhausted to hold on to. The third evening Emily actually fell asleep on the bed beside Amanda's with the phone still in her hand and Frank calling out to her. Amanda and Frank shared a good chuckle before her own head hit the pillow.

The next thing she knew, their wake-up call, unsought but arranged by their guide, drilled into her dreams. Then they were up and rushing through breakfast and out the door and onto the bus and away again.

Amanda and Emily were mostly happy with the schedule, at least at first. In the mornings they were too excited to even notice their jet lag. Their bossy guide rushed them through one site after another, and tended to talk too much when they traveled by bus. Amanda tried to shut out the droning nasal voice and concentrate on the scenery. She had never seen anything like Israel, the startling combination of past and present, divine and intensely earthbound, the eternal and the present problems, all bundled together with tension and welcome and fear and joy, every possible emotion and all the time.

But on the fifth morning Emily showed no interest in getting out of bed. "Where are we off to today?"

"The Red Sea. No, wait, that's tomorrow." Even after a cup of coffee Amanda found it hard to draw her thoughts into focus. She put it down to jet lag and an overdose of new sights and sounds. She searched her purse and found the schedule. "Today is the Jordan Valley, the Dead Sea, the museum of the scrolls, the caves, and the Engedi National Park."

"And the day after?"

"Saint Catherine's monastery," she read. "That's a long day. We leave at six, and we have a packed dinner." She refolded her schedule and glanced at her watch. "We're due downstairs in twenty minutes."

Emily did not move. "I feel like it's all been a waste."

"What are you talking about? We're covering the entire country in ten days."

Emily gave no sign she had even heard. "All the struggle and the years of dreams. Leaving Frank behind. Hauling you away from your job and Chris. All for nothing."

Amanda slipped into nurse mode. "You stay right here. I'll go fetch you something to eat, and we'll skip today's tour."

"What about little Miss Drill Sergeant?"

"You just leave her to me."

The tour guide took the news that Amanda and Emily were not joining them as a personal affront. "That is out of the question. You are letting down your friends."

"That is precisely why we are not going."

"If she is sick, we must call the doctor."

"She's not sick. She's tired."

"She can rest on the bus."

"Thanks, but no thanks." Amanda showed her most steely smile. "Have a nice day."

Amanda returned to the room with coffee, breakfast pastries, and an apple. She plumped up Emily's pillows and waited until her friend had finished eating to say, "Now, why don't you try and explain this in words I can understand."

"I didn't come here to see Israel. I came to grow closer to our Lord." She toyed with her cup. "That probably sounds silly."

"No, Emily. It doesn't sound silly at all."

"I keep feeling as though we're being rushed past the chance to dive into the real Israel."

"Why didn't you say something before now?"

"Because I like everything we're doing. It's just at night, when I lie here feeling worn out in my bones, I feel like we're running too fast to see anything at all."

Amanda took the cup from Emily's hands and set it on the table between their beds. "So what do you want to do today?"

◦

As they left the hotel Emily leaned over and kissed Amanda on the cheek. "Thank you with all my heart."

"All I did was inform Miss Bossy-Pants that we needed a day off."

"Exactly. I could never have stood up to her like that."

Amanda smiled at the thought she had done anything out of the ordinary. Standing up for people had been her job description for the past year. "Where are we going?"

Their hotel was separated from the Old City by a narrow valley. They took the path through a public garden and across the bus parking lot, climbed the hill, and entered the city by way of the Jaffa Gate. Young children plucked at their sleeves and begged them to come see the wares in various shops. Emily's eyes shone with a different light as they left the plaza and entered the narrow winding lanes. Shadows cut jagged edges from the cobblestone lane. They heard a cacophony of tongues from the people they passed. Amanda felt a giddy sense of release and did not even care when they lost their way. They asked directions time after time and took almost three hours to arrive at their destination.

There was no way of knowing whether the miniature grove across the street from the Antonio Fortress was indeed where the Healer's body had been laid to rest. Nor did it matter. The quiet garden with its carpet of fragrant pine needles was indeed the place Amanda had been looking for—only it had taken Emily's need to separate themselves from the group for Amanda to realize it.

A group of stocky women in kerchiefs and long dresses knelt in the dust before the cave's opening and traced prayer beads through rough-chapped hands. Emily and Amanda sat down on a stone bench and studied the three caves with their narrow circular openings. The stones meant to seal the burial caves were carved as great wheels set in narrow grooves, so they could be rolled into place and the family emblem applied to the wax seal. A crowd of visitors from some Asian nation—Amanda thought they were probably Filipino—began to sing. The rising chorus sounded like prayers. *Living, he loved us; dying, he saved us; / Buried, he carried our sins far away; / Rising, he justified freely forever: / One day he's coming—O glorious day.* When they were done, Amanda hummed her own song, savoring the words she did not need to speak. *The Word became flesh and dwelled among man.*

By the time they left, the morning was well and truly gone, and the afternoon heat was intense. They lunched at a falafel stand, then paused a second time for glasses of fresh-pressed pomegranate juice. They spoke only to work out their next destination, which was back up the Mount of Olives in time for the sunset. Amanda bought water and fruit from a third stand, and they left the city and crossed the Kidron Valley to climb yet another hill.

By the time they entered the ancient stand of olives, her legs were trembly and her feet ached. Emily puffed determinedly along beside her. The setting sun recast the ancient walls of Jerusalem into a crown of russet and gold. The sky was sliced by starlings who cried their shrill farewell to another day. The wind gentled, then stopped altogether. The olive grove became a haven, an open chapel to those who stood or sat or knelt and watched as the human concept of time gave way to eternal glory.

They remained there in silence until the first star glimmered in the pale blue sky. As Emily rose to her feet, she said, "Our Lord came here to beg that the cup of destiny be taken from his lips."

Something about the way Emily turned away then, almost as though she was chased down the path by her own words, left Amanda certain she knew what was coming.

Her friend waited until they had emerged from the grove and were crossing the parking lot to say, "Frank and I are facing a very serious crisis."

CHAPTER SIX

T wice each week Chris led a men's morning Bible study at their church. The previous evening he and Frank had shared dinner and watched a football game he doubted Frank even saw. At the time, he had put it down to the man missing his wife and worrying over the coming surgeries. He'd reminded his neighbor about the study and, as he had several times before, invited him to come.

Frank arrived on time, joined Chris at his table, and did not speak a word. He was not alone in his silence. Many of the regulars spent the hour sipping coffee and frowning at nothing. The group had started as a trickle, just a few of Chris's friends, then they had brought a couple of buddies, and so it had grown. That morning they numbered around seventy.

As usual Chris led them in prayer, they collected their meal and ate, then he stood up and led them in study. They'd been going through the Psalms since the recession started. So many of the verses they covered were right on target for how many of these men felt about their world.

After some concluding remarks, Chris began the final prayer by asking who had special requests. Frank followed it all with a look of somber reflection.

Normally Chris didn't speak about his own life. He felt the leader needed to remain somewhat apart and help the group focus on the needs of others. But that morning, as he watched Frank frown at the table between his hands, he took a step back and glimpsed a different perspective.

Chris had spent the entire year segmenting his life. The worries at the office and his worries over Amanda had remained isolated from each other. He did not talk about his company's plight at home. He did not speak of Amanda's crisis or the problems of his marriage at the office. If possible, he did not even think of them.

But as one person after another made their prayer requests, Chris felt almost overwhelmed by a gathering tumult. He did not want to share with this group; if he started, he would not know how to stop. His company was foundering; that morning he had to journey to Orlando for a meeting he dreaded. His marriage held a mere shadow of the passion he and Amanda had once shared. He missed his wife, and he was jealous of her time apart. He could not leave his job for a day, much less a week and a half. More than anything he wished for the closeness they had once known. He wanted to feel as though she traveled for them both.

Frank raised his hand and the room snapped back into focus. "This probably isn't done, a visitor asking for prayer help from strangers."

"There aren't any rules, Frank. You're welcome to say whatever you want."

"My wife and I have a problem child. She was the brightest star in our family, and then one day when she was nineteen the flame went out. We learned later she had gotten into drugs."

The man's voice was flat as pounded tin. There were a few murmurs of sympathy from the group, a few refocusing of distant gazes as Frank went on.

"She's promised to go straight so many times I stopped counting. Three years ago she came home, claiming it was all behind her. A week later she vanished again, taking all my wife's jewelry with her." Frank gripped his hands on the table, one with the other, the skin of his face so taut it was pale as old bones. "And now she wants to come home again. She's pregnant and she's living just south of Orlando all on her own. The baby is due in three months. She tells us the problems are all behind her. Again. She wants us to help give them both a stable environment."

Chris waited until he was certain his neighbor was done, then asked, "What do *you* want, Frank?"

The man's gaze tracked around the room, as though he had trouble identifying who had spoken. "I don't want to argue anymore. Not with my wife. And not with my little girl."

A voice from the back of the room said, "I hear you, man."

Chris found it hard to shape the words he had spoken so often to this group. "It's important that we try and focus on the positive. Especially when our world is clouded by worries. Give ourselves something to aim for. Try and determine a course that is in harmony with our hearts."

"What I *want*." Frank's voice sounded strangled. "I can't tell you how alien that sounds. You might as well be speaking Greek."

Chris felt the man's emotions resonate through his entire being. He saw the fear etched into Frank's features and had to force his response around the emotions that clenched his throat up tight. What he was asking of Frank was precisely what he needed to do himself. "Try. Please."

The room watched his struggle in silence, ready to wait with him all day. Finally Frank said, "I want to do the right thing. For Emily, for our daughter, for the baby, and most of all for our marriage."

Normally Chris led the prayer time. But today it was hard enough just asking, "Who wants to start us off?"

As one man after another of the group stood and prayed, Chris clenched the lectern and listened to his own internal prayer. He needed to rediscover the positive, search out a genuine purpose to this time apart. Do more than just survive another day, another meeting, another crisis at work. Give a significance to these lonely hours.

The answer came to him with the group's final amen. Not a solution to his problems, but rather a way he might give meaning to this one day. Look beyond his trials and focus on the unseen, at least for this one morning.

As they walked outside, Chris thanked his neighbor for coming and asked, "Where is your daughter living?"

"I don't know exactly. All she said was she's working part-time in some church's youth center. First Methodist of Kissimmee." Frank must have seen something in Chris's face because he asked, "You know it?"

"I've heard of them, sure." He wouldn't tell Frank anything more. Not yet. "They've got a good name for helping the community."

Frank crossed the parking lot. "I wish you could know what it's meant to me, being here today."

"I wish you could know what it's meant to me, having you come."

Frank started to respond, but instead he merely beeped open his car, tapped his hand on the roof, and declared, "It's a good morning to be alive."

Chris waved his neighbor away and found himself thinking about Amanda. For once the hope of returning to the tender relationship they had known seemed real, a flame that fed upon the light he had seen in Frank's face.

❧

Avery Electronics was started in the early days of World War II. Kent Avery, the current CEO, was the fourth of their family to run the group. They specialized in electronic systems for military jets. But government projects were drying up, so Chris had been reassigned to develop business within the commercial markets. He and his new division had been more successful than anyone could have hoped. But not enough to keep the company going. Since taking on his new role, Chris had attended several board meetings. He knew the numbers. The company was poised on a knife's edge.

The lawyers Chris was meeting in Orlando represented a Brazilian company called Campaeo. They were the largest manufacturer of planes and jets in South America, and were setting up a new factory in Melbourne Beach. Even before the facility was built, they had a reputation throughout central Florida.

Initially Kent Avery had considered the Campaeo offer a lifeline. But most of the people who had done business with Campaeo shook their heads when asked and said, never again. Chris knew this because he had sought them out. He'd brought in several respected local business owners, all of whom described Campaeo as the poisoned chalice. Hearing this, Kent Avery refused to meet with the Brazilians himself. He feared that if he were there, even with Chris at his side, he would agree to anything in order to keep his company going. So he sent Chris to make the journey alone.

The attorneys representing Campaeo occupied the top three floors in one of downtown Orlando's pricey high-rises. People in fine suits rushed about, talking power and money and offering him brisk, knowing smiles if they looked his way at all.

Forty-five minutes later than scheduled, Chris was finally ushered into the conference room. He declined their offer of coffee and looked at the people lining the table's opposite side. There were six of them, two women and four men. Chris assumed the man at the far end was actually from Campaeo. He had heard this was one of their tactics, having a director attend these early meetings but masking his real position. Giving him a chance to study the prey before pouncing. The Brazilian man was sleek, wearing a shiny tailored suit and flashy tie, with piercing eyes like a vulture's.

Evan Crouch, the senior attorney, cleared his throat and said, "We were expecting Mr. Avery."

"Kent couldn't make it."

"Then we'll need to reschedule. I'm sorry you made the trip for nothing."

"He won't be able to make it then either."

The attorney started to look down the table but checked himself. "Surely the amount of business my client is proposing to do with your company deserves more respect."

Chris fastened his gaze upon the Brazilian and did not reply.

"Because really, this offer of yours is not at all what we had expected. It will need to be renegotiated from the first clause to the last. Such discussions require the presence—"

"The offer stands. Take it or leave it."

"Is this some sort of joke?"

"Do I look like I'm joking to you?" Chris kept staring at the Brazilian. "Let me tell you what is happening. You focus on companies that are desperate. You make a huge offer of new business. You get the best possible deal, then you string out payment. You increase the amount of the order so they don't complain too loudly over not being paid on time. When they're really desperate, you offer to buy them out. For pennies. And because you've wrecked their finances, some of them have no choice but to agree."

The lawyer coughed. "This is slander."

"It's slander if it's untrue." Chris drew the contract away from the senior lawyer and slid it down the table to the Brazilian. "The price is the price. You set up a letter of credit. You pay on time."

The meeting came to a close, but Chris carried no satisfaction away from it. And yet, as he took the elevator back to the parking garage, he knew he had done the right thing. A small part of him wished he could return upstairs, sit back down, and sign a contract that would guarantee his company's survival. Instead he forced himself to start the car and drive away. Because the truth was inescapable. Upstairs in the lawyers' conference room was a deal that represented nothing more than groveling and vanquished hopes and defeat.

And he had another task awaiting him, the one that had come to him during the morning prayer time. A purpose that added a genuine sense of meaning to the day.

Chris took the airport highway south into the neighboring city of Kissimmee. He knew Kissimmee Methodist Church. Twice each year that congregation partnered with his on mission trips. He headed south and west, following the main arteries leading around Orlando's southern residential developments. He entered Kissimmee at the opposite end of the sprawling township from Disney and drove through neighborhoods filled with cheap hotels and low-rent apartment blocks and liquor stores and fast-food chains. Flashy billboards could not mask the shadows and the grime.

He pulled around the main church building and parked in front of a day care and crisis center run by the church. The steeple rose to his right, a defiant gesture against the desperate need and angry scowl that blistered many of the young faces he saw as he rose from the car. The asphalt basketball court was occupied by a group of Latinos playing a team made up of African Americans and whites. All the kids were scrawny and feral. The play was rough, the language rougher.

The low-slung building had probably once held offices. He pushed through cracked glass doors and entered an impossibly cheerful lobby. The walls were plastered with hand-painted posters shouting messages of hope and love and sobriety and salvation.

"May I help you?"

"My name is—"

"Chris?"

He did a swift double take at the woman he vaguely recalled. "Jackie?"

"I thought I recognized you. How are you doing?"

Jackie had been a nurse at the Melbourne hospital, who three years back had felt a strong calling to go into full-time ministry. Now she served on Kissimmee Methodist's staff. She and Amanda had remained fast friends—until last December, when Amanda had basically severed all but the most critical ties.

Chris found the day only held room for the truth. "Well, I'm not so good."

"I'm sorry to hear that. Would coffee help?"

"Coffee would be great. But I don't want to take you from your work."

"My work is all about meeting people's needs." She pointed him to the reception desk where a large man was watching him with careful eyes. "Everyone has to sign in. We deal with some pretty hard cases around here."

"I saw some hard cases out there on the basketball court."

"No, those kids are doing all right. Some of their families are still living out of their cars, but we're working on that. Basically, if they're in our teen center or out there on the court, they have a solid chance of making it. The lost ones are those who don't come around, or don't come back."

Jackie led him into the cafeteria. Everything had a makeshift air, including the mismatched chairs and the scarred table. But it was all spotless, and the air carried a slight fragrance of disinfectant. A number of the tables were occupied by people cradling cups and talking in low tones. Jackie poured them two cups and pointed him to an empty table by the back wall. "How's Amanda?"

"At the moment she's in Israel."

"Is that why you're facing difficulties?"

"No, not at all. She went because a friend's husband is ill and couldn't make the trip." He took a sip. The coffee was excellent. He told her about the meeting he had just left, and the problems that tainted his day.

As he talked, Chris found himself missing Amanda with a biting intensity—not the woman he had seen off at the airport, but the woman he had married. The Amanda whose bright eyes shone with love and drank him in. Who gave him such open-hearted affection he felt ashamed sometimes at how feeble his own love was in comparison. He longed for the way they used to talk back when they spent hours on the patio watching night draw its velvet drapes across the Florida sky. He had not realized until then just how much her distance had cost him, especially now, with so much going on. Chris did not so much finish his tale as run out of steam.

Jackie gave him the respect of a few silent moments just to ensure he was done, then said, "You know what we're doing here?"

"I assume it's a rehab center."

"That's right. And one of the problems we deal with is the fact that the drink or the drug is not the critical issue. In order to deal with the drug, the patient has to deal with the underlying issue. When you met with that rotten company today, you were dealing with your underlying issue. Quite successfully."

"I don't see how you can say that when Avery is still threatened by bankruptcy."

"The company's troubles are what's on the surface. I'm talking about the turmoil you're feeling down at a deeper level." She slid her mug to one side. "Sometimes the only way to see the truth is by turning a secret corner. Looking *beyond* the thing that's dominating your vision. In your case it's the responsibility that you feel for your company. You're sad because a real solution to your company's problems, a genuine offer, would be such a great thing. But this wasn't, was it? Real?"

He shook his head. "No. It never was."

"That's what we're forcing people to accept here. That going back to whatever it is that's wrecked their lives, no matter how desperately they'd like to have one more taste, one more high, will only return them to the same ruined state. Until they turn away and look beyond, they will never see the true salvation that awaits them."

He found himself growing uneasy under the glow of her smile, as though she was congratulating him for something he had not done. "I'm here for a neighbor. His daughter is an addict. Supposedly she's cleaned herself up."

"But he's heard all that before, right?"

"All too often."

"And he thinks she's here?"

"She gave him this address in a letter she wrote. She also said she was pregnant."

Jackie's face brightened still further. "Frank and Emily Wright are your neighbors?"

"Yes."

"Wow. Talk about miracles."

"Frank doesn't know I'm here. Matter of fact, I don't even know their daughter's name."

"It's Lucy, and you are an answer to a prayer." She rose from the table. "Come with me."

CHAPTER SEVEN

The teen center was housed in a former mini-mart on the basketball court's other side. It was good that it was well separated from the other church buildings, because the place greeted Chris with one solid wall of noise. Rap music blared while the crowd yelled and jibed around a pair of battered pool tables. The side wall held an array of electronic games, all of which banged and chimed and yeowed and blasted. Through a glass partition Chris could see two rooms. One contained a dozen or so computer stations and more empty desks where kids studied. Compared to the front room, the study center was an island of sanity. The other rear room was the office, where a woman sat behind a desk and talked to a sullen teen sprawled on a stained sofa. One glance was enough for Chris to know the woman was Frank and Emily's daughter.

Jackie rapped on the glass, then waited for Lucy to look over and wave them in. When she shut the door behind them, he heard Lucy say, "Go tell Ramon he better lay off the little kids."

The boy rose to his feet, shifted his oversized jeans, and said, "You gonna talk to the cops?"

"No, Anthony. *You're* the one who's going to talk to the detective, just like we agreed."

"But you'll be there, right?"

"I said I would be. Now, you want to make the call to social services?"

"No, man, I don't want to say another *word* to that lady."

"But you have to. Either that or she's going to take you from your mother and put you in foster care. So who's going to pick up the phone, you or me?"

"You do it."

"'Will you do it, please, Lucy?'" Lucy said.

He repeated the words, though it cost him. Then he slipped past Chris and Jackie without acknowledging their presence. Lucy said, "You're welcome, Anthony."

He shut the door hard enough to rattle the glass.

Only then did Lucy focus her attention on them.

Jackie said, "This is Chris Vance. Chris lives across the street from your folks."

Lucy's only response to the news was to drop one hand to her extended belly.

Jackie asked, "You mind if we sit down?"

"Sure thing."

Chris unfolded a metal chair leaning against the side wall. He had no interest in coming within ten feet of that sofa. He seated himself across the desk from Lucy and studied her intently. The lady had packed a lot of hard living into her twentysome years.

When Jackie finished with the introductions, Lucy asked, "Does Pop know you're here?"

"No. Nor does Emily."

That surprised her. "Why not Mom?"

"She's in Israel."

"So she finally got to go. Good for her. How come Pop's not with her?"

"He's facing a health issue."

Her face tightened with concern. "Bad?"

"He needs two hip replacements."

"So what did he tell you—he doubts his little girl is finally sober?"

"Not exactly." Chris had no problem being straight with her. "He wants to be certain you won't hurt them again. I know there's no way I can find that out for him. But I thought maybe . . ."

Jackie said quietly, "You did the right thing."

Lucy's chin trembled momentarily before she brought herself back under iron-hard control. "He's right to worry."

Jackie said, "Lucy has been on staff here for a year and a half. How long ago did you graduate from our rehab center?"

"Almost three years." Her eyes glittered overbright with unshed tears. "I wound up here after I wasted my way through the money I got from hocking Mom's jewels. She told you about that?"

"Your dad did. Yes."

"One of the things they teach us here is facing up to the low points, and using them as a driving force to never fall again." She cocked her chin toward the ceiling, as though trying to dislodge something in her throat. "Even so, I feel branded by the memory of what I did."

Jackie said, "When she graduated from our rehab program, Lucy moved into the apartments across the street. They used to be a motel. We converted them into studio apartments where we house families for up to six months while they try to straighten out their lives. Lucy started volunteering here. She turned out to be a diamond in the rough. The kids respond to her like no one we've ever seen before. She sees things before they happen and helps the kids out there get straight and stay straight. They feel safe here. Because of her."

"I believe you," Chris said.

"About a year ago Lucy married an instructor at the rehab center," Jackie went on. "Unfortunately, he responded to the news that she was pregnant by going back on his drug of choice. We did an intervention. We gave him the ultimatum. Enter rehab, straighten out his life, or leave. We haven't heard from him since."

"I'm sorry," Chris said.

"The important thing is that Lucy has remained on the straight and narrow. She's been clean for almost three years. She studies the Scriptures and she makes them live for the kids you see out there. She teaches them the message of eternal hope. She makes Jesus live for them." Jackie's gaze rested calmly on the other woman. "And she is my friend."

Lucy asked, "Will you take a message to Pop?"

"Of course."

"Tell him I want my baby to know the best childhood anyone could ever have. Which is what I got, and then threw away." There was a coppery tint to her eyes and her voice. "Maybe my daughter will be smarter than I was. I hope so."

Chris rose to his feet. He looked at the two of them and said, "I'll tell him. Whether he hears me or not is another matter. Either way, I'm glad I came."

CHAPTER EIGHT

Amanda and Emily were still talking about it the next morning over breakfast. The buffet was a perfect representation of the hotel's international visitors and contained everything from pickled herring to waffles. Over it all was draped an aromatic veil, filling the room with the scents of mint tea and chicory-laced coffee and hot chocolate with cinnamon. Each morning Amanda walked down the line, savoring the sights, before taking her standard fare of fruit and yogurt.

"Can I tell you what I think?" Amanda asked.

"Why do you think I brought it up? I've been wanting to talk about this ever since I heard."

"How long have you known?"

"Six weeks."

"Frank must have spent these last six weeks in knots."

"Actually, Frank didn't hear about it until three days before we left."

"You didn't tell him until we were leaving?"

Emily shook her head sadly. "It was a terrible thing to do. But I couldn't bring myself to mention it."

"What did he say?"

"That he wished I hadn't told him at all."

The news pushed Amanda back in her seat. "Frank Wright is the nicest, kindest man I have ever known. He's what every grandfather should be. I cannot imagine him ever saying such a thing."

"Well, he did. What's more, he meant it."

"I still don't see how Frank can shut out his own daughter, especially when she's soon to have a baby."

"You have no idea what that girl has put us through," Emily replied. "If you had even the faintest inkling, you'd be standing there beside Frank, barring her from ever setting foot inside our home."

Amanda cut off her response at the sight of their tour guide approaching the table.

"I suppose it would be acceptable to the rest of our group if you rejoined us today."

Amanda did not need to ask Emily's opinion. Her friend's expression said it all. "Sorry, but we'll be on our own again."

The tour guide was an angular woman in her late fifties and spoke with an accent Amanda had decided was either German or Austrian. She held herself with Teutonic stiffness, especially when displeased, like now. "Again you wish to let down your group?"

"We're not letting anyone down," Emily replied. "We're doing what we came to Israel to do."

When she started to object, Amanda said with a steeliness all her own, "Good-bye."

Emily idly watched the group depart the breakfast room. "Do you know, talking this over with you has done me a world of good."

"I don't see how. I haven't said a thing of any use."

"It's allowed me to share the burden."

"You know, it's crazy, but hearing all this has forced me to look beyond my own troubles. For the first time in, well, much too long."

"You were surrounded by other people's troubles every hour of the day at the hospital."

"That's right, I was. And they never touched me. Nothing has. Until—" She was interrupted by the sound of her cell phone ringing. She fished it from her purse and checked the readout, but all it said was "International." "If it's the hospital, they're going to be glad they're close to the urgent care unit."

But when she answered, she heard Chris say, "We need to talk."

They had returned to their room and were ready when Chris phoned them back, this time through the hotel switchboard. Amanda put him on the speaker phone, then listened as Chris related his visit to the Kissimmee church. She had not been able to squelch the gasp of surprise at the news that Emily's daughter worked in the outreach center with Jackie.

❧

The air seemed impossibly bright when they finally left the hotel. Amanda told herself it was silly: the weather was exactly as it had been every day since their arrival, crisp and dry in the mornings, hot by noon, blistering by afternoon, and dropping to near freezing within an hour after the sun went down. The night winds seemed to blow straight through her clothes, no matter how many layers she wore, rather than take the longer route around. It was almost eleven before they finally rounded the hotel and crossed the narrow defile to old Jerusalem. She felt very comfortable in a light cotton pullover. They walked in silence, both women filled to the brim with thoughts they needed time to digest.

Emily spoke first. "Who is this Jackie?"

"She was a nurse at the Melbourne hospital. Awhile back she told everybody she felt called to go into full-time ministry. Most of the staff figured she was going through an early midlife crisis. We stayed in touch. At least we did, until . . ."

Amanda walked on in silence, reflecting on how she had turned her daughter's stillborn birth into a life change of her own. She felt no need to defend her actions. This was not about blame or even regret. This was about honesty.

As they approached the hordes of tourists pouring out of the buses parked by the Jaffa Gate, Emily said, "I've studied the map. We can walk around the Old City to where we're going. But it will take longer."

"Who cares how long it takes? We're on no one's schedule but our own."

They followed the sidewalk down the escarpment and around the perimeter of the Valley of Tombs. They arrived at yet another parking area filled with buses.

"This is something I've wanted to do all my life." Emily pointed to the steep-sided hill that rose on the parking lot's opposite side. "This is the Temple Mount. Solomon's Temple was up there. Now all that's left is the wall you see over there."

On the lot's other side, behind barriers and a concrete plaza, loomed a wall of stones big as buses that literally supported the hill. Amanda felt a faint thrill over the presence of living biblical history. "That's the Wailing Wall, right?"

"Yes. It's all that's left of the original temple structure. Up there, on top of the hill, the compound now holds a mosque and a museum. The ultra-religious Jews won't go inside the compound because they don't know where the Holy of Holies was located, and they might step on the forbidden space. So they come and pray here."

Amanda had seen enough pictures for the scene to hold an almost familiar feel. The plaza and the space before the Wall was packed. Many of the people teeming around wore the long beards and wide-brimmed black hats of the Orthodox. Suddenly she felt self-conscious. "The only people I see praying up there are men."

"There's a separate area through the door to the left for women to go and pray." Emily fished in her purse. "This has been a destination point for pilgrims for over a thousand years. The idea is to write out a prayer and slip it into the stones."

A childlike wonder grew in Amanda, an intense desire to get this right. "What do I say?"

"The prayer needs to be something you've carried in your heart since you started the journey."

Amanda pointed to an empty concrete bench fronting the barrier. "Can we sit there and give me time to think?"

"Absolutely," Emily replied. "But you don't need to think. You need to pray."

᧤

Beyond the barrier stretched a featureless area paved in new stone, perhaps a hundred feet at its widest point. Over to their left was a narrow walk guarded by a booth and numerous guards, forming the only entry into the hallowed ground. Two open portals marked the corner where the path met the wall, one for women and another for men. According to Emily's research, the men also had a chamber where the wall stretched under what was now an extension of the hillside. They had both seen photographs of men standing and praying and reading their prayer books as they swayed.

Amanda pulled the leather-bound book from her purse containing the Psalms and the New Testament. Even this was cause for shame. Here she was, praying at what had been a pilgrimage site for ten centuries, and she had to start by coming face-to-face with how little she had either prayed or studied over the past twelve months. She had gone through the motions, attending church and going to a women's Bible study occasionally. But it was all external. Inside she had felt nothing.

Now she sat in the bright sunlight and stared at the text in her hands and realized why. To feel anything at all would have meant giving in to the anger and the bitterness. Instead, she had pushed all emotions away, hidden them down deep in the secret recesses of her wounded heart.

Sitting there on the hard stone bench, surrounded by strangers and noise, Amanda did not feel angry anymore. She felt raw and open and empty. She looked at the pen and the notepad on the bench beside her, and wondered if maybe what she really needed to write was *I'm sorry*.

She felt a swooping sense of rising away from where she was and where she had been for the past year. Part of her remained

seated there beside Emily, who had started sniffling while leafing through the pages of her own Bible. But another part was
up very high indeed, far away from the regret and the year of
wounds and stress and sleepless nights. Now she saw with a clarity far more piercing than this sunlit desert day. She was able to
envisage the prayer she would have written, had she been able to
sit here at any point over the past twelve months: *Turn back the
clock. Make my baby live.*

But there was no going back. Time only moved forward. It
had been moving all year, hard as she had tried to peel back the
hours and change the life she had been given, and make her baby
arrive happy and whole and alive.

Martha would have been one year old today.

They'd given her Christopher's mother's name. Amanda
had considered it one of life's great gifts, coming to know her
husband's wonderful mother before Alzheimer's had stolen away
her mind. So Martha had been their first choice for the baby,
the only name either of them ever really considered. Amanda
recalled the day with vivid clarity, coming home from a company party, celebrating a new account Chris had landed, one
with great hope for new growth and new jobs and a new future.
There in the car he had asked her thoughts about a name for
the baby; when she told him, he had to pull to the curb because
he was so happy he could not keep the tears from blurring his
vision.

But Martha had never taken her first breath. And the new
client had gone bankrupt. And all their hopes had been lost to
a rising storm.

Amanda cleared her eyes and looked again at the Wall rising
before her, with the rows of bearded men reading and swaying

and gesticulating and praying. She saw the slender slips of paper wedged into the cracks. And suddenly she understood.

It came to her with a silent shout, as clear as a thunderous explosion, one powerful enough to resonate through her entire being and shake away the veil of regret. Life had dealt her a harsh and undeserved blow. She had survived. Now it was time to move on. The question was, move on toward what? That was the only choice she had. She could remain shackled to all that was past. Or she could face all the uncertainties and fears and doubts that a new day might bring.

Amanda picked up the pad and pen and wrote her prayer.

Father, give me the power to live a full life.

Give me the strength to be a loving wife.

Awaken in me a new hope.

CHAPTER NINE

B ut as they stood and started toward the entrance, they were halted by what awaited them on the other side.

"This is *not* what I came here for," Emily declared.

Visitors were checked through the security perimeter one by one. They then passed down a narrow open-sided corridor before approaching the Wall itself. At this point, young men in black suits and beards and wide-brimmed hats or yarmulkes stepped forth and welcomed them. They were courteous and intelligent and they spoke a variety of languages. And they stayed with the visitors, and they talked and they talked. They only departed once a gift was made, and if the payment was given while the visitor was still inside the security area, another young man instantly pounced.

"It is kind of a circus," Amanda agreed.

Amanda and Emily watched the bearded, black-clad men swirl and swoop on yet another couple entering the compound.

"I came here to *pray*," Emily said. "Not to be accosted by bearded guides."

Amanda came up with a possible solution. "I could go talk to one of them back in the parking lot. Ask if they would sort of keep the others away if we agree to pay them."

A voice from behind them said, "No, no, that won't do. It won't do at all."

Amanda and Emily turned to find themselves looking down at a diminutive Israeli woman. "Why not?" Amanda asked.

"Because the young man will take your money, is why not. They'll take as much as you can give them, more than you want. Then when you've paid, they'll push you to hurry. And since they're forbidden from touching the women, they will press you with their voices." The woman was as wrinkled as a sun-bleached prune, with glittering eyes almost lost in the folds of her face. She waved her cane in front of them. "Shoo, shoo, they will tell you. Go and hurry and get away, so I can go find another to pay me."

"But that's awful," Emily said. "Why do they let this happen?"

"They? Who is 'they'? Those men, they are the they."

"I'm sorry, what?"

"They are all studying for the rabbinate. You understand, rabbinate? They are young and they have families and they are hungry. They spend all their time pulling at their beards and arguing over books and praying. Then they come here, they say, to pray. And yes, of course, they do pray. But after, they tell the tourists, welcome, welcome, here is the Wall, and this is the history, and now you pay me and go, good-bye, and here comes another."

Amanda interpreted, "They have every right to come and pray at the Wall, and they use this as an opportunity to pester visitors who don't know any better."

"Is what I said, no?"

"But what do we do?" Emily demanded. "I've waited all my life to come here and pray too. And I don't want somebody knocking on my elbow and telling me it's time to leave!"

"I already say, they don't touch the women."

"You know exactly what I mean."

The woman was not the least put off by Emily's irritation. Her wrinkles rearranged themselves into a very ancient smile. "From where are you coming?"

"Florida."

"I hear is very nice, this Florida." She gestured with one swollen hand. "Come."

As they approached the security perimeter, Emily and Amanda tied colorful scarves over their hair. The old woman nodded approval. Just before the checkpoint at the Wall's entryway, the first of the young rabbis moved forward. The old woman snapped a single word and the man backpedalled away. Twice more it happened as they approached the Wall. Each time the old woman served as their protector.

They entered the dark corridor leading to the women's section and were instantly surrounded by a quiet noise, like the sound of a rushing stream: women's voices, hundreds of them, joined together in solitary prayer. The flood of sound carried such force it seemed to sever all connection to the outside world.

The chamber was long and broad and softly lit. The only adornments were fragments of stone set into the other three walls, riven with faint traces of ancient script. Benches were scattered about the chamber. Women lined the space before the wall, some standing with hands clasped and eyes shut, others reading from holy books and swaying slightly as they chanted. Amanda and Emily shared a smile of quiet delight.

Amanda stayed in front of the Wall, reading from her little book and praying, until her feet hurt. When she turned away, she expected to find the old woman gone. But there she was, seated on a bench, reading from a tattered book of her own. Amanda walked over and saw that the text was in Hebrew. She sat down beside the woman and waited until her head turned her way to say, "I can't thank you enough."

"You are pleased with this, your visit?"

"It is everything I hoped for and more."

"Good. Then I too am pleased. *Nu*, you will perhaps do me a favor?"

"Of course."

She held out her hands, the joints swollen and twisted with arthritis. "It is not possible for me to shape the words. I have a paper, I was going to put it in the Wall. The Holy One, he knows what is on my heart. But it would be nice to have the words written there." Again there was the rearrangement of wrinkles. "One can never tell. Perhaps he likes reading things, yes?"

"I would be happy to help."

The woman reached into the pocket of her dark jacket, shiny with wear and washing, and pulled out a folded slip of cheap paper. "You have a pen?"

"Yes."

"Write these words. *Heal Rochele.*"

"I'm sorry, how do you spell that name?"

"Rochele. Rachel. Heal Rachel."

"All right. I've written it. Anything else?"

"That is enough. That is why I came. To pray for the child." But as Amanda started to rise, the woman reached over to halt her. "Perhaps there is another. But I have no more paper."

Amanda settled back and reached into her purse for her pad. "I do."

"What do you think, will the Almighty dislike me for coming with one request and asking two?"

"I sure hope not. I came with nothing and I've written down a lot."

A stronger tremor entered the old woman's voice. "Write this, then. *If you will not heal the child, give me the strength to survive her passage.*"

CHAPTER TEN

A s Chris turned into his drive, he was greeted with the humid fragrances of ocean and seaweed. The street where he and Amanda lived was only four houses long. Three properties ran down each side, and the two owned by the Vances and the Wrights shared the narrow circle at the end. Chris loved their cul de sac and how it cut them off from the beach hordes. Yet they were close enough to smell the salt every time the wind blew from the east.

He loved driving from October until April with his windows down. He loved being in a beachside town that had remained tight-knit and conservative and strong enough to withstand the tourist tides. He loved his job and his company. He loved his wife.

He cut off his motor and remained where he was, staring at his garage door and the lights to either side of his front porch. They were set on a timer, something he had thought was silly when Amanda had insisted upon it, but now considered a boon, as it kept him from arriving home to a dark, empty house. He listened to the crickets and the gulls and thought how wonderful it was, to be alive and in love with his wife and living here.

He heard footsteps through his open window and turned to see Frank approaching. "You aiming on coming over, or do I feed your steak to the dogs next door?"

Chris remembered. "You invited me for dinner."

"It wasn't an engraved invitation, but yeah, that's right."

"I totally forgot." Chris rubbed his face. "What a day."

Frank's grin reflected the doorlights. "One of the many reasons I'm glad to be retired."

Chris rolled up his windows and fell in beside his neighbor. "How late am I?"

"None that you'd notice. I fired up the grill awhile back and just let the coals cook down." He glanced over. "Did I disturb a worry session?"

"Actually, I was just giving thanks. Something I used to do all the time, driving home, knowing Amanda was there waiting for me. It's been so long . . ."

Frank didn't speak as they rounded the house and entered the screened lanai containing a miniature pool and an indoor-outdoor seating area. "Make yourself comfortable. Pitcher there has lemonade and pomegranate juice made up fresh. Emily's favorite. You want anything else, help yourself in the kitchen."

"This is fine." But he didn't move. Now that he was seated, even reaching for a glass was more effort than he cared to make.

Frank made a process of fanning the grill. "You want to talk about your day?"

Chris knew he needed to tell Frank about going to meet Lucy. Instead, he thought back over the meeting that had started less than half an hour after he returned from Orlando.

"My company's CEO asked me to attend the board of directors meeting."

"Is that good?"

"Hard to say."

The board had asked Chris endless questions about Campaeo and why he had talked to them as he had. Chris assumed a complaint had been lodged at the highest levels, most likely through the Orlando lawyers. He should probably have been fearful for his job, especially with cutbacks looming. But after the meeting in Kissimmee he had remained filled by an unusual sense of clarity and peace. So Chris had calmly reported his research into Campaeo, describing the US executives who had been only too happy to recount their frustration over the Brazilian way of doing business.

He had then recited from memory the process through which he had come up with the figures for their own bid, and his insistence upon having payment secured up front. Kent Avery had not spoken once. When Chris was done, the board asked for a few clarifications, then looked at one another, as though a secret signal was being passed, before asking him to remain for the rest of their discussion. Chris was ready to leave; he had a dozen critical issues waiting on his desk. But he had phoned downstairs, explained the situation, then sat there and listened to them worry for another half hour before his impatience boiled over.

No one had been more surprised than Chris himself when he had stood up and respectfully told them that this was the time for decisive action. There were a number of issues that required their attention. Worrying about things they could not control helped no one. The company's employees were counting on them for leadership. Which, with all due respect, he had not heard much of since entering the room. Then he had left. And driven home. And given thanks along the way. Which was astonishing, really, since he had probably just signed his own dismissal notice.

"No," Chris said. "I really don't want to talk about it at all."

"Fine by me." Frank laid the two strip steaks on the grill. "Medium rare okay with you?"

"That would be great."

"I've been sitting here thinking about my sister."

"This is the sister you and Emily came down to look after when she got sick?"

"I only had the one." Frank poked the steaks with a long fork. "Elaine was one special lady. My mom and dad worked all the time, so she basically raised me. She was nine years older. Looked after me and the house both. She never married."

"She taught high school, is that right?"

"For a while, then she went back for her master's in education. Ended up principal of the Melbourne Beach high school. Kids loved her. Filled the church for her funeral." He turned the steaks over. "Lucy was her favorite. Almost like the child she never had."

Chris sat up straighter. Waiting. Ready.

"The way Elaine used to go on about Melbourne Beach, we thought she was nuts. Well, not nuts, I guess. But she loved it so much we figured she'd grown blind to the downside. We liked it well enough when we came for visits. But it was only when we came down to care for her that we saw she'd been right all along. Just like Elaine, looking after us to the very end."

Chris watched him bring out a salad bowl from the kitchen. "Can I help?"

"You stay right there." Frank returned for cutlery and plates and napkins, then used a glove to bring out two baked potatoes, which he cut lengthwise, coated with butter, and set on the grill beside the steaks. "Lucy was the child we had after losing our little one. You heard about that?"

"Amanda told me. I'm so sorry."

"I don't know what Emily would have done if Lucy hadn't come along. She was the perfect baby. Nothing can make up for losing a child, but Lucy filled our hearts, I'll tell you that much. She gave the days meaning." Frank laid the meat and the baked potatoes on the plates, set them on the table, seated himself, and offered grace. "Dig in."

Chris ate with gusto, giving Frank time to make peace with his memories. It was only after they had cleaned up and were seated back at the table, watching the night capture the back garden, that he finally said, "I went to Orlando today. I had a meeting with some lawyers."

"How'd that go?"

"About like I expected." Chris took a hard breath. Now that the time had come, he wondered whether he had made a terrible mistake, doing this without first asking permission. "After that, I went down to Kissimmee. I know some people at the church where Lucy serves."

The crickets filled the void until Frank asked, "You saw her?"

"I did, Frank."

"You talked?"

"For over an hour." Chris glanced over and saw how Frank's shoulders and neck were bunched and knotted, like a boxer waiting for the next unseen blow.

Frank's voice was so tight his throat rattled. "Tell me."

~

Chris was still on his first cup of coffee when Frank called. "You having another breakfast at the church today?"

"Every Tuesday and Wednesday."

"Mind if I come along?"

"Of course not, Frank. You'd be welcome." Chris hung up with the question still unanswered. As in, why Frank had not said anything about this the previous evening. Why he waited until six in the morning. But Chris saw no need to ask anything. Not while the dawn was flavored by the conversation he'd had with Amanda. About her visit to a wall.

Of course he'd heard about the Wailing Wall. He'd seen photographs of the dark-suited, bearded men standing and praying before the ancient edifice. What astounded him was how Amanda had spoken about her visit there with Emily. She had not so much related their experience as sung the words. He'd listened to her describe the old Israeli woman and prayers they had written on slips of paper and stuck into cracks in the wall. But what he had fastened upon was the joy in his wife's voice. Something absent for so long he had almost forgotten how it sounded. Which was both beautiful and sad. Because if there had been any one way to describe his wife in their early years, it had been joyous.

Which was why Chris wound up speaking as he did at the breakfast.

Their church had been built back in the sixties, when water views were still something people thought they would always enjoy. Like most structures dating from that era, the church placed a road between itself and the waterfront, so the city was responsible for upkeep after the hurricanes tore through. The buildings were low and stucco and connected by lawns and covered walks. The cafeteria itself needed updating, as did most of the other facilities. But out the rear windows, beyond the palms and oleander, sparkled the pristine blue of the Inland Waterway. Birds flocked to the sheltered cove just beyond the church's fishing dock. The air through the open windows was sweet and filled with the songs only heard in the weeks leading up to Christmas.

What made this morning special was the appearance of Kent Avery. Over the four years the men had been meeting, quite a number of Avery employees had joined the group, but Chris could not have said whether his boss even knew about these meetings. But there he was, seated at a table with a group of shop workers, who seemed as surprised as Chris to see the company president there. Chris could not hear their words, but he could see the way conversation started and ran around the table, with Kent listening attentively and nodding to each person in turn.

At their own table things were a bit different. Frank brooded in silence, eating nothing and cradling a cup of coffee he did not touch. Chris was not sorry when the meal was done and it was time to say his few words.

It was not until he was standing at the podium and midway through their prayer requests that he decided to talk about Amanda. "Most of you know about our having lost a baby this time last year. She was stillborn, which in some people's eyes means the child was never really ours. And that's true enough, in the sense that we never fed her or cared for her or heard her cry in the night. But she was ours just the same. My wife and I lost our little girl, and we have spent the past year grieving.

"Some of you met Frank, my neighbor and friend, here yesterday. Wave your hand, Frank. Last week his wife and mine went off to Israel together. At the time I thought it was a good idea without really understanding why. It was when we were talking on the phone that I understood.

"We're all going through tough times. Many of us are facing some really hard choices, at work and in our private lives. But the thought I want to share with you this morning is this: there are more important things than our jobs, or troubles, or even our homes and providing for our families. There are eternal things, the matters of heaven. And the purest and most powerful way this presents itself here on earth is in love. The love we share with our families. The love we show to the family of believers. This morning I want you to think about one person who needs your love, who needs you to be there for them in a way that maybe you haven't. Maybe you have forgotten something, or neglected a duty, or been blind to a need or an opportunity. This person may have forgiven you the neglect, because they know what you're facing. But Jesus urges us to turn away from fear and pain and frustration, and toward love. I believe he wants us to repair our love, or strengthen our love. I'm encouraging you this morning to think of one simple act that represents your heart for a new hope . . ."

Chris stopped, defeated by his inability to express what was on his heart. "Someone want to lead us in prayer? . . . Okay, great."

He bowed his head with the others, his face flaming with the ham-handed way he felt he'd spoken. He rarely talked to the group off the cuff, and usually felt afterward that he hadn't communicated well. He suspected that his discomfort today was at least partly due to Kent's unexpected presence, which only made his shame the greater. Especially when he lifted his head at the end of his prayer and found his boss sitting there, staring blankly into the distance.

When the group broke up, Chris watched as both Frank and the company's president started toward him. He thought several others also were aimed his way, but as soon as they saw Kent heading over, they veered away. When Frank saw that Kent was going to reach Chris first, he frowned and backed up, clearly irritated that he had to wait.

If Kent Avery noticed how most of the people in the room were watching them, he gave no sign. "We need to have a word."

Here it comes, Chris thought. "Sure thing."

"Do you want to wait until we get back to the company?"

"Here is fine." Chris settled into the chair he had just vacated and asked, "What can I do for you?"

As if he didn't know.

Kent settled across from him, laced his fingers together on the table, and said to his hands, "I'm tired, Chris."

The words were so far from what he had expected to hear, Chris could only think to say, "Excuse me?"

"Tired. Worn out. I haven't had a decent night's sleep in . . . I don't even know. Too long. I'm sixty-seven years old, and I'm tired."

Chris felt as though his mind was suddenly caught on an overtight leash. It skittered in one direction, turned, and ran off in another. He couldn't tell what was happening. Kent's refusal to meet his gaze only made it worse. Maybe the president was trying to cushion the news that the board was going to fire him. Maybe the man had decided to close the company, fold up his tent, and leave. Or maybe they were going with the Brazilian's offer after all, or were going directly to them with a chance to be bought out, or . . .

"Four generations," Kent said, still talking to the table by his hands. The bald spot at the crown of his head caught the overhead lights. "You know about my son."

Chris nodded. Kent's only child had never shown any interest in the company, other than spending his inheritance as fast as he could get his hands on it. Chris realized Kent could not see his motion, but just then he could not find any words.

"You won't remember this. But you'd been with the company about four weeks when your boss, old Larry Frame, had you deliver the presentation on our newest client."

I remember, Chris wanted to say. Because he did. Vividly. But he remained silent.

"I watched this kid get up there and wow the management team with his enthusiasm. I saw the delight you had in being where you were. I heard you talk about our company, our clients, our future. And I wished . . ."

"You can go ahead and say it," Chris managed to say. He did not recognize his own voice.

"What?"

"I shouldn't have spoken yesterday like I did. The board wants my head."

Kent cocked his head to one side. "You think I came here this morning to fire you?"

"I probably deserve it. But they needed to hear it, Kent. The company needs the board to lead."

"No, Chris. I'm sorry. But you're wrong."

"Excuse me?"

"They need *you* to lead them."

He felt hammered back in his seat. He knew he was gaping at his boss and couldn't stop.

"Oh, I'll grant you a couple of the older fellows in there didn't take kindly to your opinions. But most of them felt exactly as I did. Which was, I was right to suggest the change. And you were the right one to lead us forward."

"What change is this, Kent?"

"Two months ago I knew I wasn't up to finding a way free of this mess. I don't know if anyone is, I'll tell you that up front. You might be out of a job before you can settle into your new office." He stared into the distance. "Nine weeks ago I had a serious attack of chest pain. I was rushed to the ER, they ran the tests, told me I'd had a bad case of gastritis, possibly was starting on an ulcer. But before I heard the diagnosis, the only regret I felt was over not having spent more time with my wife."

Chris nodded. He knew that sentiment all too well.

"Basically what I felt most was relief. That the stress and strain were over. That I could lay down this burden for good."

"I understand," Chris murmured. And he did.

"So I want you to take over." Kent leaned forward, closing the distance between them. "I'm sure of one thing. If anyone is capable of building a future for Avery Electronics, it's you."

"Kent, I don't know what to say. This was the last thing I expected."

"I got to tell you, it's good to be able to hand somebody a reason to be happy for a change." He settled back and looked around the room. "I never had much time for God and such. My grandfather was a rigid old hidebound Methodist, and my father rebelled with every ounce of his being. I guess I just followed in his footsteps. You never met my dad, did you?"

"No." His voice sounded distant, like he was listening to another man speak. "He passed the year before I joined the company."

"I thought the world of my old man. It's shamed me no end, not being able to carry on, make him proud."

"You haven't let anyone down, Kent. Not me, not your dad, and not a single person who works here. You're the finest boss I could ever imagine having."

Kent continued to scan the empty cafeteria. "I got to tell you, I was moved by what you said. And by the way people responded." He rapped his knuckles on the table, almost as though he wanted to cut off that topic before it could go any further. "I'll stay on as CEO. But as of this moment, you're president of Avery. Now I want you to skip out, lie low, give the company time for the news to filter through. Don't show your face around the plant until next Tuesday. We'll have a formal announcement. Then I'll walk you through the books, get you ready for the quarterly meeting with the outside auditors on Wednesday afternoon."

"Kent, thank you, really . . ." Chris swallowed hard. "I'll give it my best."

Kent rose to his feet. "You always have."

CHAPTER ELEVEN

C hris walked out of the church at a steady pace. He knew because he could see his reflection in the glass wall overlooking the parking area and the oleander border and the shimmering water. But inside he was nothing but a balloon, bounding down the hall on an unseen string, striking the walls and ceiling and floors. Not so much giddy as disconnected. He saw Frank standing outside by his car, kicking at a pebble and talking on the phone. Chris knew he had to go speak with his friend, and he suspected whatever was said would bring him back to earth. Back to the problems and the reality of everything this day held. Pity the lightheaded moment could not have lasted a bit longer.

The sun was December mild, a brilliant light scattered by the morning haze. The church's Christmas decorations glittered and spun in the breeze. Chris heard someone call his name and he waved in response. Just another friend from church, whose day was not overwhelmed by the most unexpected of news.

Him. Chris Vance. President of Avery Electronics. It was an aspiration he had never dared dream.

Frank continued to kick at pebbles on the asphalt as Chris approached. "I need to know what you think I should do about Lucy."

Chris did not speak. He took a long breath. Savoring the moment just a bit longer.

Frank took his silence as reluctance to talk and said, "I spent all night thinking about what you told me. And you were right to go, because I know now I couldn't have handled it. And I believe what you said. At least, I believe that's what you saw. But I just don't . . ."

Chris looked at the man. He knew what Amanda said about him. How Frank Wright had the biggest smile and the most brilliant hello of all the hospital volunteers. How he offered a concerned word to all the frightened arrivals. How he made them feel welcome. How he promised them that inside were healing and hope and the best that modern medicine could offer. Chris felt as though the morning light illuminated the moment in a way that only his heart could see. "You're worried about how Emily is going to respond."

"I'm worried about us," Frank agreed to the pavement at his feet. "The worst arguments we ever had were over Lucy. We've been so happy here. I don't want to lose that."

"I called Amanda after I got back from Kissimmee. She put me on the speaker. Emily listened in."

Frank kicked harder. "And?"

"She's worried about *you*. All her concern is over how you're going to manage this."

Frank released a breath so big his entire body deflated. "I don't deserve her."

"I feel the exact same way about Amanda."

"Will you tell me what you think I should do?"

"Yes." Chris thought about Lucy. A hard-edged woman, but sober. And alert. And doing some amazing work with some kids for whom she was the only hope. "I think God is calling you to make a trip to Kissimmee."

Frank had gone so still he appeared to have stopped breathing. When Chris finished speaking, he remained like that, frozen in the morning light. A cardinal shouted a greeting. Frank jerked slightly, as though the song had shaken him awake. "I need to go see her."

"I think so."

"I should do this before Emily gets back."

"Probably so."

"Will you come with me?"

Chris saw the fear and the dread on Frank's creased features. It pained him to see the man's customary cheerfulness overwhelmed by events. "Yes, Frank. Of course I'll come."

∾

They decided to take Chris's car, so first Chris followed Frank back to their street. He tried to reach Amanda on the drive home, but he was put straight through to her voice mail. And the news about his promotion was not something he would leave in a message. Scarcely had he pulled into the drive when his assistant phoned with the news that Campaeo's lawyers urgently needed to speak with him. Chris had the impression she already knew about his promotion, and that repressing her excitement was like trapping steam in an overheated kettle. But he didn't say anything, so she didn't either.

She patched the attorney through, and when Chris identified himself, Evan Crouch said, "I specifically asked to speak with the company president."

"That's me."

"But Kent Avery's secretary insisted upon—" There was a pause. "Excuse me?"

Frank opened the passenger door, saw Chris was on the phone, and hesitated. Chris waved him in and said to the phone, "I was appointed this morning."

The man took his time responding. "You're the president of Avery Electronics?"

"I am."

"Then congratulations are in order," he said sourly.

"What can I do for you?"

"We need to meet."

"I can tell you everything you need to hear right now and save us the time," Chris replied. "Our offer stands as it is."

But the lawyer was insistent. "You owe it to your company to hear what we have to say."

Chris reluctantly agreed, then called Kent Avery to report the conversation. In truth, he was hoping for a reason not to go.

"Follow your best instincts," Avery replied easily. His boss already sounded like a different man. "If there's anything to be gained from them, you'll find a way."

Chris cut the connection and turned to his friend. "Something's come up."

Frank tried for resolute and failed. "I can handle this on my own."

"No, I just need to swing by these lawyers in Orlando before we head to the church." As they started across the causeway bridge, Chris explained what was happening.

Frank heard him out and said simply, "Kent Avery chose the right man for the job."

"I might be the briefest company president in Florida's history."

"You might. But that's less important than being certain everything possible is being done to save the company."

"Frank, you're a good man and a better cheerleader. But you don't know a thing about my company or me as an executive."

"I know how you are seen by the men in that morning group. I see how they look up to you. How they trust you. With their lives." Frank nodded slowly. "And those people you've been feeding from the Word, they will share their confidence with everyone else."

Which was why, when they arrived at the glittering Orlando building that housed the lawyers, Chris was smiling.

∽

Frank declined his offer to wait in the coffee shop on the office building's ground floor, so Chris left the older man seated in the car and headed for the elevators. To his surprise, he felt none of the tension he had carried with him on his last visit. Even when the lawyers kept him waiting twenty minutes, he found himself content to sit and reflect upon the day. He felt as though something kept the world at a safe distance. Even now, surrounded as he was by the prospect of his company going under, and being forced to wait until a group of high-priced attorneys offered him a false lifeline, he felt protected.

He was struck then by the conviction that Frank was downstairs praying for him. That was why the old guy had wanted to wait there in the underground garage. So he could offer Chris this incredible gift.

The sense of being sheltered was so strong Chris could sit there across from the receptionist's desk and respond with prayers of his own. He did not close his eyes. He had no desire to draw attention to his deed. He prayed for Frank and the coming meeting. He prayed for Amanda and the prayers she had placed in the Wailing Wall for them both. He prayed for their marriage and their future. And he prayed for his company.

A gradual realization welled up inside him. Chris did not so much stop praying as turn the process around. He no longer spoke. He listened in prayer. He saw how his determination to separate his family life from his business problems was only partly driven by a desire to protect Amanda. In truth, he did so because it *suited* him. He wanted to be the strong one. The man who was in control of his job and his destiny. And the hardest part of this entire episode was learning that he was *not* in control. There was almost *nothing* about the situation that was entirely his to manage. And yet, throughout it all, he had been so very reluctant to release his clenched grip and allow God to take over. He wanted to *fix things*. It was his nature. Only now, as he sat in the reception area and waited for the lawyers to call him in, did he see how important it was to let go. Not merely of this meeting. But of his desire to segment and control.

As Chris felt his internal barriers crumble, he realized that this was the true definition of wisdom. To see his earthly situation through God's eternal gaze.

Chris found his comforting shield remained in place even when the lawyers launched into their pitch. He continued to view the process from two entirely different perspectives. On the one hand, he listened as they listed the benefits that would come to Avery Electronics through working with their Brazilian clients. He heard how any sensible executive would be willing to bend on the few points that separated him and his company from a huge new deal. And on another hand he saw that his former bitterness was based largely on the baggage he himself had carried into this project. Ever since the run-up to the previous Christmas, when that first prospective client had gone bust and Amanda had lost her baby, he had entered into every possible deal like he faced a pitched battle. Not allowing himself to see how the tension had eaten at him, or the burdens had weighed him down.

The senior lawyer clearly saw he was not getting through. "I'm sorry, Mr. Vance, are you even hearing what I'm saying?"

"Every word."

"Because I keep expecting you to respond with more than a smile. This is an incredible offer we're making."

"Is it? Let me put it to you as plainly as I know how. The deal with Campaeo Aviation could be a lifesaver. But only if it is *real*."

"I can assure you, sir, that this proposal is absolutely—"

"Just hear me out. From where I'm sitting, *real* includes a price that will grant us the chance to make a small but reasonable profit. Real also includes getting paid *on time*." Chris pointed at the deal memo he had brought along the last time. "We have cut our cost structure to the bone and priced accordingly. That won't change. And neither will the terms. A real deal is one where we are paid for what we deliver. *When* we deliver."

"But surely you understand that there has to be give and take—"

Chris rose to his feet. "Gentlemen, this is my first day in a new job. To be perfectly honest, I wish I could be spending it somewhere else. Where there is a chance of a *real* deal, one that will offer my company *real* hope. Good-bye."

He strode from the conference room and passed through their offices. He did not wait for the elevator. He took the stairs. They were concrete and unadorned. His footsteps echoed through the chamber as he crossed the underground garage to his car. When he slipped behind the wheel, he asked, "Were you praying for me?"

"It was the least I could do after all you've done to help me and Emily," Frank replied. "How did it go?"

"Better than I could ever have hoped." Chris started the car. "I needed to draw a line in the sand. For my company and our future. And I didn't know it until I was upstairs."

"Well, all right, then."

Chris looked at the man seated beside him. He saw the nerves and the tension. He saw how Frank carried a similar bundle of past problems and worries and pain. "You ready?" he said. "Let's go see Lucy."

CHAPTER TWELVE

When they pulled into the church parking lot, Frank emerged from the car like a stiff old man. Chris watched him limp across the parking area, totally ignoring the young people playing basketball. He knew Frank's attitude had nothing to do with the place or the young people, and everything to do with the woman who waited inside.

Chris had phoned twice, first before leaving Melbourne Beach and then again when they left the downtown garage in Orlando. Jackie was there to greet them. She kissed Chris on the cheek, then turned and said, "And you must be Frank. I'm Jackie, Lucy's supervisor."

"Nice to meet you." Frank's voice was almost robotic. "Where's Lucy?"

"Hiding in the youth center. As nervous as I imagine you are." Jackie ushered them back into her office. "I volunteered to serve as a sort of go-between. I hope that's okay."

Frank loosened enough to reply, "Chris told me a little of

99

what's happened since Lucy showed up. I appreciate everything you've done for my daughter."

"She's a wonderful person, and a real boon to our efforts around here."

"I got to tell you, that's not something I ever expected to hear, especially in a church."

"I understand."

Frank eased himself down into a straight-back chair. Chris leaned against the back wall, wanting to give the two of them some room. Frank said, "I don't even know what to expect."

"Or why you're here, I imagine." Jackie's own chair creaked loudly as she leaned back. "At the risk of repeating what Chris may have already told you, let me give you some background. Lucy first came through our rehab program three years ago. At the time we asked her if there were any relatives we needed to alert. She gave us your names. You were up in Ohio then, if I remember correctly?"

"Outside Dayton," Frank confirmed.

"Right. Lucy said she didn't want you notified unless there was an emergency. She said she had put you through enough. She also said she'd promised to straighten herself out and failed too often to count."

Frank huffed softly, but did not speak.

"I have to tell you, I liked her from the start. We get a lot of liars in this place, a lot of people who are good at telling others only what they want to hear. Lucy was different. She had hit rock bottom and she didn't like what she'd found there. She graduated from the center's program and got a job at a local fast-food place. She attended AA meetings every night. She joined our church. She joined our Bible study. She went to night school.

And she started volunteering with the kids you saw on your way in. She has a real gift, by the way. She can reach kids that I would have long since given up on. They trust her in ways that would just . . . well, they trust her. And she loves them. She gives it to them hard and straight, but with a sense of uncompromising love. We watched her for over a year, then we designed a position for her. She's been full-time on our staff for almost two years."

Frank covered his eyes.

"She met her husband through us, I'm sorry to say. He was a charmer. Won us all over. But something about the pressure of becoming a father just pushed him over the edge. None of us saw it coming. When he took off, we were worried we'd lose Lucy as well, but she's held to the straight and narrow." Jackie raised her hands. "That's as clear as I know how to make it. Your daughter has given her life to Jesus, and he has given her a reason to live. Sure, she could fail again. We all could. Lucy is giving it her best. I'm proud of her. When she told me she was thinking about contacting you folks, I told her it was time."

Jackie waited. There was a considered patience to her, as though she had been in this position before. She did not move, she did not press. When Frank finally regained control, she said, "Ready to go see your little girl?"

~◊~

Chris watched through the glass partition as Jackie brought father and daughter together, then slipped into the study room with her. Together they watched Frank and Lucy through the window.

"How's Amanda?" Jackie asked.

"She sounds great. Tired. They're trying to cram all of Israel into a week and a half."

"Un-huh. Her first trip, right?"

"Yes." Chris watched Lucy scoot her chair around the desk so she could sit with her father and not have the desk between them. Frank's features looked rigid, but he made no move to draw away from her. Chris asked, "Are you all right with them getting together?"

Jackie glanced at him briefly, then went back to watching. "Are you kidding? I live for this."

Frank said something that caused Lucy to reach over and take his hand. He jerked at her touch but did not pull away. He kept shooting his daughter tight little sideways glances. Like he was afraid.

"So we're not observing them because you're worried."

"No, I'm not worried."

Lucy started talking then. Frank's face gradually began to relax.

Chris asked, "Then what are we doing here?"

"There just aren't enough happy endings in this work. We deal with impossible situations. We pray for miracles. Sometimes they happen."

"And you think this is one of those times."

"I don't think. I know."

In the other room Lucy continued talking. Chris watched the tension gradually ease from Frank's frame. He was studying his daughter full on now.

Chris found the silence comforting. He needed a bit of distance himself, from the day and all that was going on. He found that his mind did not return to the surprise announcement, however. Instead it swept across the sea to Amanda and the incredible change he was hearing in her voice. Somehow it all felt tied together. The trip the women were on, and the trip he and Frank had taken. Two completely different journeys, yet somehow they transcended distance and time and were bound together by something far greater than he could ever hope to understand.

Jackie said quietly, "Moments like this are why I do what I do. Watching a kid who has every reason to hate open the Bible, then listening to him talk about love and forgiveness. Standing beside addicts as they graduate from rehab, and hearing them thank God for bringing them to us. Having a day when we get a homeless family out of their car and show their kids a room with a real door and a real bed where they can sleep from now on."

Chris was watching her now. "It sounds to me like you've got a world filled with miracles."

"Not enough." As Frank and Lucy rose from their chairs and embraced, she reached over and took his hand, all without glancing away from the sight, without even blinking. "Not ever enough."

CHAPTER THIRTEEN

T he journey home started in silence. Chris had no problem with not talking. The day resonated with a palpable force, and he needed time to digest not the events but the realizations. As they waited for the last light before entering the expressway, he tried phoning Amanda once more. When it went straight to her voice mail, he simply told her everything was fine and asked her to call.

"You and Amanda headed anywhere for Christmas this year?" Frank asked.

"We were supposed to. But we'll probably stay put. How about you and Emily?"

"The kids and their families joined us last year. This Christmas they'll be with in-laws. We didn't plan it this way, but it works out for the best, since I'll be able to recover from the surgery in peace. You have family up in Virginia, right?"

"A lot." Chris merged into the highway flow. "To be honest, I don't know if we'll ever go back. Not after last year."

Chris found himself talking easily about growing up as the youngest of five children, the closeness they felt for one another, the pain of dealing with their beloved mother's Alzheimer's and subsequent death. And the quarrel with his sister Claire.

He spoke for the first time of their arrival at his sister's home on Christmas Eve. He had not said a word about it before then to anyone. He had in fact done his best to forget the events had ever happened.

Up to the day of their arrival at Claire's home, Amanda had been briskly handling the loss of the baby. She had insisted upon going back to work. She wasn't sleeping, neither of them were. But other than that and a new sternness she showed to the world, she seemed to be getting on with life. Until Christmas Eve when she had walked into Claire's home.

The house was filled with family and noise and laughter. Children of all ages were everywhere, playing board games in front of the fire, fighting over controls to the television and the Xbox, inspecting the wrapped presents, reading a book in the corner, helping in the kitchen. The lights on the tree and framing the living room entryway had cast Amanda's features in a sickly pallor. Then suddenly she had started wailing. Great, heaving sobs that sent her crashing to the floor. Several of the children started crying with real fear.

Chris picked his wife up and carried her to the bedroom. When her weeping continued without pause, Claire's dentist husband had finally given her a sedative. Even with that she had needed over an hour to calm down. In the middle of the night, she woke up and declared they had to leave while everyone still slept. Chris recounted that awful drive, eleven hours seated beside a woman whose face had been transformed by raw pain. He had never felt so helpless in his life. Amanda had spent a week moving around their home like a zombie, not leaving, not even going out into the backyard.

"I remember," Frank said.

"Really?" Chris demanded. "How?"

"Emily wept when she saw her get out of the car that day. Not for Amanda. Remembering." Frank shook his head. "Why did you even take her to Virginia?"

"Claire really wanted us to come, and Amanda thought it would do her good."

Frank was quiet for a couple of miles. "Maybe it did."

"Did you hear a word I just said?"

Frank glanced over. "The pain had to come out sometime."

Chris started to object, then remained silent.

Frank started talking then. He told about growing up in a house where his father's arrival was a reason for celebrating. His dad was a long-distance trucker, gone for a week or so at a time. Frank described his mother as an angel who bound their family together with not just love but constancy. She was a steady hand, an army brat who had gone to nine different schools in six countries, who had loved her parents but vowed to give her own children what she had never had, a home that was theirs for life. She had stayed in the home to her last breath, surrounded by the clan she had founded and whose roots remained deep in the rocky Ohio soil.

When Frank finished, the two men drove in silence for a time. Chris started to ask about Lucy, what had gone on in the room and what Frank might do next, but something told him to wait. One glance at his friend's face was enough to know Lucy was there with them. Her presence filled the car.

The light was almost perfect when Chris arrived at the shoreline an hour beyond sunset. The sky was a spectacular array of rose and gentle golds. The beach at low tide was wide, the exposed sand hard and compressed and almost dry. The sun sank low into the sky as a few couples watched the fading light and a man threw a Frisbee for his dog. Chris knew several of the people and waved in greeting, then began to run south, away from the boardwalk and the last tourists and the high-rise condos. A couple of dogs raced after him until their owners called them back; he ran on alone.

He often found himself praying in such times, quick snippets of thoughts, sometimes little more than images with no words at all. A picture of Amanda looking at him, the love light strong in her gaze, and a swelling urge to give thanks for the miracle that brought her into his life. A quick prayer for all her unfulfilled dreams, the needs that she seldom spoke of, especially now when his own world was so pressured.

This was followed by the image of Kent's face as he was seated across the cafeteria table that morning. The relief he showed when Chris accepted. Of course he had said yes. What else could he say to such an incredible offer? He pounded next to the booming surf and repeated the title: President of Avery Electronics. He had a fleeting sense of understanding Kent's reaction, and saw how it must have felt, wrestling not just with the idea of stepping down, but with the fact that a four-generation legacy was coming to an end. Chris felt another upswelling of emotion and knew he had to go in tomorrow and thank the man again. Because it wasn't just a job and it wasn't just a responsibility. The simple fact that Kent had felt so relieved when the deed was done left Chris convinced that it was the right decision for both of them.

If only he could do whatever was required and come up with an answer to save the company from the wrecking ball.

Which was good for another prayer.

He stopped then and stared out over the ocean, where the first eastern stars were just coming into view. He stretched his thigh muscles, then turned and started back.

He wondered about telling Amanda about his promotion. Whether it might be better to wait until her return, and they could savor the moment. He asked himself what she might prefer, and liked the fact that he had asked this at all.

It was when he climbed the stairs from the sand to the boardwalk that the idea came to him.

He liked it so much he smiled his entire way down the side road to the main street, then along the sidewalk to their cul de sac. He checked the time and decided that it wasn't too late. He phoned the shop down the road and caught the woman just as she was closing up. He apologized for the hour and asked, "Do you have any idea how I could send some flowers to Jerusalem?"

CHAPTER FOURTEEN

C hris called out a greeting as he entered the house without knocking. He found Frank in the kitchen cutting vegetables and took over making the salad. Frank started the grill and set the patio table. The two of them moved around each other in comfortable ease. As Chris poured them glasses of lemonade, Frank set the plate with two steaks on the sideboard and said, "I've been thinking. You need to call your sister."

Chris stopped blowing on the coals and turned around.

"By now she's full of regret over what she said last Christmas. And she doesn't know what to do because she can't say she's sorry."

Chris swiveled the lid over the coals to let them burn down. "Why can't she?"

"Because she's human. Because you scared her to death. You asked her what she would feel like if she lost a child. It's the truth she's spent the entire year avoiding, ever since Amanda broke down." Frank took his time settling into a chair. "Your sister's a believer, right?"

"Yes."

"So she likes to think God is going to protect her from all the hard knocks. Then here comes Amanda. Married to the brother she loves. A good woman doing good work at the hospital. A believer like her. And Amanda gets hit by your sister's worst nightmare. How can she explain this? The simple fact is, she can't. Nobody can."

"I never thought of it like that."

"You've been dealing with your own impossibles this year. Amanda and the company and your own grief. It's a wonder you remember your name." Frank waved toward the kitchen. "Go give her a call. Tell her it's fine. You love her. Amanda is healing. Your sister needs to hear that from you."

❧

Claire's voice came out low, subdued. "I'm glad you called."

Chris could hear a frantic caterwauling in the background. "What's going on over there?"

"Just the normal. The animals grow restless at feeding time."

He disliked hearing his sister down, and even more the fact that he was the cause of it. "I shouldn't have said what I did, Claire."

"No. You shouldn't have." She sighed noisily. "But you did. And I haven't been able to stop thinking about it."

"I didn't mean to scare you. I just wanted you to understand what Amanda has been going through."

"How could I not understand? I *saw* it."

"If you understood, you wouldn't be pressing us to come up this Christmas."

"I just thought—"

"Amanda needs to come to this in her own time, in her own way."

"We miss you. It won't be Christmas without you."

"Yes, it will." He fumbled for something positive and could only settle on, "We'll call."

"So you're really not coming?"

He found himself filled with a genuine remorse. But this was the right decision. "No, Claire. Sorry. But no."

A bit of the bossy tone returned. "I can't believe I'm letting you get away with this."

"You're not *letting* me do anything. I'm doing this for my wife. Whom I love very much."

"Nobody could ever push you into doing anything you didn't want to do. It used to get me so angry."

"And it didn't do you any good, did it? So don't start now."

There followed a sort of huffy silence, one that Chris recalled vividly from his growing-up years. Then, "I love you, my hard-headed brother."

"Take care, Claire. I'll call you when I can."

CHAPTER FIFTEEN

Amanda and Emily entered the main plaza fronting the Jerusalem bus station and were instantly enveloped by a crowd. The people jostled and talked and pushed. They were not being impolite, Amanda realized; it was just the nature of the Jerusalem bus terminal. Frenetic, a bit tense, and very loud. She stopped four people before one of them took the time to read the name on her slip of paper. The woman called to a man in a bus uniform, giving the village name a guttural lilt that Amanda could not hope to emulate. The officer gave her and Emily a typical underhanded wave, gesturing for them to follow. They ran and pushed as he easily slipped through the crowd, not once looking back to see whether they kept up. He pointed them to a bus and moved instantly away, not granting them a second to thank him.

The driver informed them that they wouldn't depart for another fifteen minutes, so the two women walked over to a neighboring stand and bought plastic cups of fresh-squeezed orange juice.

"I never thought I would find a place that offered anything as fine as Florida juice," Amanda declared. "I was wrong."

Emily had been silent through the walk to the terminal, almost withdrawn. "Are you sure you don't mind if I don't go with you?"

"Of course not. To be honest, I'm not sure why I'm going either. It's unlikely I'll discover something the Israeli doctors missed."

"But you should go. I just feel like I need some time alone to absorb everything that's happened."

Emily had been acting strange ever since getting off the phone with her husband.

"Will you tell me what's going on?" Amanda asked.

"Frank went to see Lucy. With Chris." She glanced at her watch. "They should be on their way home now."

"Why didn't you say something?"

"I just did."

"You know what I mean."

Emily gave an almost dream-like smile. "I prayed for this, and now it's happened."

"That was what you wrote and put in the Wall? That Frank would go see your daughter?"

"Of course not, silly. I asked for peace in our family. All our family." She sighed. "Frank has been like a powder keg ever since Lucy got in touch."

"That must have been very hard on you."

"Frank is so protective. He knows how much all this has hurt me. Lucy was the daughter we had after we lost our little one. She has been special to me ever since."

"Which only made it hurt worse when things went wrong," Amanda finished. "Poor Frank."

"After she stole my mother's jewelry, he barred her from ever setting foot in our house again. But it wasn't because of the theft. It was because he couldn't stand to see her hurt me anymore." Emily smiled. "I never thought this day would ever come."

Amanda took hold of her friend's hand.

"Will you say a prayer for us?"

"Of course." Amanda spoke the words with eyes open, not giving a thought to all the people surrounding them. There they sat, two Western women at an aluminum table in the noisy station. Another bus rumbled away. Around them people chattered and rushed. When she finished praying, Amanda continued to hold Emily's hand. She found herself thinking back on her own little slip of paper, writing the words and fitting it into a crack between the big stone blocks. She wondered if there was any chance of her own miracle appearing like that.

⌁

As the bus trundled through the town of Bet Jola, Amanda had the sense that she had entered a different Israel. The quiet little town was less than twenty miles from the center of Jerusalem, yet worlds removed from the touristy bustle. She stared out the bus window at a seedy, rundown city, but what she saw was the world of normal Israelis. People looking for work and holding down jobs and doing the best they could for their families. Arabs and Israelis alike strolled the streets. There were a number of women and even more children. But between these isolated pockets of activity, the place held a remarkable sense of timeless silence.

The name of the woman they'd met at the Wailing Wall

was Miriam. She lived in a small house of her own, one of few in a village dominated by apartment blocks. Hers was the oldest structure on the street, a flat-roofed building of one story with a waist-high wall bordering the street. The concrete and stone wall was whitewashed and gleamed in the sunlight. The front windows were barred, the door made of nail-studded wood.

Amanda rang the bell and waited. She could feel eyes watching her, but when she turned and looked she saw no one.

Miriam opened her door and nodded her satisfaction. "You came."

"Thank you for inviting me."

"It is good to offer a stranger the hand of peace, yes? Come, come. There is a little angel I would like you to meet."

❧

What had undoubtedly once been a small and rather ordinary home of indeterminate age was now a welcoming palace of bright colors. The stone floors were layered with soft carpets. The walls were all freshly painted in rose and coral and lavender and sky blue, then adorned with smiling butterflies and great sunflowers and rainbows. The furniture was pared down to child-size, small tables with chairs and benches to match. The tiny entryway was lined with shelves and hooks. The living room's rear wall held a basinet and changing area and all the accoutrements any infant station might require.

As Miriam led Amanda through the kitchen, two young women in kerchiefs paused in their meal preparation to smile and greet her. Through the open rear doorway Amanda saw an unexpectedly large garden, which had been turned into a playground.

The infants' play area was under a broad canopy with gauze netting. The sandbox was huge and was set within an emerald green lawn. It was the nicest patch of grass she had seen in Israel. The swing sets and slides were set back behind a hedge of blooming flowers that also bordered a netball court. In that way, there was not one play area but three, all sectioned carefully from one another, to match three age groups, all playing happily in their own areas. The surrounding wall was ancient, made of stone up to about shoulder height, with a newer addition of stone and concrete that rose to well over Amanda's head.

Miriam then led her into a back bedroom that had been turned into a nursery. A number of little pallets were piled in one corner. Shelves were filled with toys and stuffed dolls. All of them looked to have seen many years and many little hands. Two of the three cribs were occupied with sleeping infants.

The rear windows were covered with gauze-like drapes. The filtered sunlight turned everything the color of soft rose. The lighting was so dim Amanda did not notice the little girl at first. Then she saw the little hands go up.

A child was playing quietly in a corner between the cribs. As soon as she spotted Miriam, she extended her hands, pleading silently to be picked up. Miriam walked over and lifted the little girl, who nestled into the nape of the woman's neck as she had clearly done so many times before. From this place of safety, bright, dark eyes watched Amanda.

"This is Rochele," Miriam said. "Can you say hello, my little one? No? Well, never you mind. There is nothing the matter with silence."

Amanda smiled at the child, but at the sight of a stranger the girl hid her face behind Miriam's hair. Amanda suspected the child already had a lifetime's experience with the things doctors and nurses hid behind their smiles. "How old is she?"

"Two years and two months. She is very small, yes?"

"There can be a great deal of difference in body types. But, yes, she does appear somewhat undersized."

And frail. There were all the telltale signs of poor health, the pallid features, the slack skin. And, yes, she was very small. "She receives enough nourishment?"

"We are constantly pressing her to eat more."

Amanda caught the defensive tone. "I wasn't talking about the child's time with you here. I'm sure you do the best you can with all the children in your care. I meant at home. Is there money for food, and is she cared for by her family?"

"This little one could not be more loved or cared for. The problem is not her food."

Amanda was tempted to check on the types of food Rochele was being fed. But she caught the manner in which Miriam held the child. This woman had seen too much of doctors as well. Their suspicious questions, their desire to assign blame, their callous manner of mistrust. "I am sure you and Rochele's family do everything possible to keep this child healthy."

Miriam visibly relaxed. "And yet I fail. We all do."

"She looks all right."

"She is. Today. This hour. Everything is good. But only because we keep her sheltered, away from the others, eating her little nibbles every two or three hours, feeding her as we would a baby bird. And she eats like one, don't you, my precious darling?"

Miriam carried the child back into the living room, and

Amanda followed. The kerchiefed woman tending the stove turned as they passed and crooned at Rochele, who responded with a shy smile. Miriam seated herself on the divan and let the child slip between her knees, where she stood with the uncertainty and imbalance of someone half her age, suggesting a severe lack of muscle development.

"Can you tell me her symptoms?"

"So many symptoms. So much this darling girl must endure. You will be here for hours."

"I have hours."

"*Nu.* She even looks at one of the others playing outside, she is ill. She breathes dust, she is ill. She plays with a cat, the same. She loves my cat but she cannot touch it, not even for an instant. She watches the world through a window, and she grows up alone."

"Her parents?"

"Her father is gone from us, may he rest in peace. A good man, but also not strong. His lungs. He was young when he was taken, only thirty-five. He and his wife emigrated from Tunis. A few Jews still live there, not many. Once there were forty-three synagogues in the city, now there are two. So when the Arab Spring opened the borders, they came. Rochele arrived four months after her father died. We called her a gift from heaven. But now, with these aliments . . ." Miriam breathed once, a rattling sigh. "The mother, she has suffered too much."

Amanda gave that a long moment, then softly pressed, "What precisely are Rochele's symptoms?"

"She never has the normal child's ailments. With this one it is never just a cold. Her fevers, ah, you must see them to believe. One moment she is fine, the next her fever rises to a hundred and two, a hundred and three, and still it rises. We bathe her in ice water, and slowly it goes down. Then there are the coughs. How such a tiny one can cough like this . . . it hurts me to watch her try and breathe."

Amanda reached out one finger like she was approaching a shy kitten. The child watched her with solemn eyes but did not back away. Amanda stroked the soft dark hair, the face. Rochele was truly a beautiful girl, with the calm resignation of someone far older.

Miriam said, "Tell me what you are thinking."

"It sounds like an autoimmune disorder, which is very rare in infants but not totally unheard of. Has she always been this way, or did it come on her gradually?"

"The doctors, they all ask the same. And the answer is, from the very first day the little darling has not been well. She could not drink her mother's milk. So they put her on soya."

"Severe allergic reactions to a number of various . . ."

Amanda stopped talking because the child reached for her.

It was the most natural thing in the world to take Rochele in her arms. She felt the girl's arms slide around her neck and one hand take hold of her hair. The little face nestled into the point where Amanda's neck met her shoulder. Then Rochele sighed. A tiny wind against her ear, and she went still.

For one as creased by time as Miriam, the old woman had a most remarkable smile. Her mouth shifted only a little, and yet every line on her heavily wrinkled face turned upward. "This one has a new friend."

Amanda patted the girl's back and breathed in the sweet smell.

"She never lets anyone hold her," Miriam said. "Me, the one you saw cooking, her mother. No one else."

The cook must have heard them, for she popped her head into the living room. Her eyes went wide, and she called out the door and gestured. The other young woman came running, and she too stood amazed. They jabbered at Miriam, who said, "The one you see by the door, she has been with me since the first day Rochele arrived. Never has she been allowed to do what you are doing."

Amanda knew she should be asking and observing. But just then only one thought came to her. "I lost a child."

The creases resettled into their familiar lines. "When was this?"

"Almost exactly a year ago. She was stillborn."

"Did she have a name, this one?"

"Martha." With a start, Amanda realized it was the first time she had spoken the name since the day she lost her. The sense of release was so strong, she said it again. "Martha was the name of Christopher's mother. Chris is my husband."

"And so you could never hold this child, this beloved Martha. And so your arms are still empty." The words carried a pragmatic calm. "Rochele feels this."

"You really think so?"

"Those who have hurt and grow from the pain, these are the ones to trust when your burden is heavy. Who is to say that a little child with a golden heart cannot also feel another child's absence?"

Amanda felt the child stir and let her slip down to dangle by her knees as Miriam had done. She kept one finger extended so Rochele could grip it for balance. They were still seated like that a half hour later when Rochele's mother arrived.

Alathea was a Sephardic name, rich in Tunisian Jewish heritage. Miriam explained this to Amanda as Alathea cooed over her daughter. Amanda guessed the mother's age to be in the early thirties, not far from her own. But one brief glance at Alathea was enough to know this woman had carried more than her share of burdens. She looked permanently weary. Her face was being redrawn into lines of hardship. Yet there was a tensile strength to her slender form, a quiet determination to her dark gaze. And the love she showed to her little girl made Amanda's eyes burn.

Alathea worked as a cleaning woman in one of the local businesses. Her only son was twelve, and handsome like her late husband. Miriam translated Alathea's words in a soft murmur.

Amanda said, "I worked as the chief critical care nurse in a maternity ward. You know, before."

The wizened face opened wide. "This is true, what you are telling me?"

"It was. But I haven't been back in the ward since last year. I tried. Once. The week before I came to Israel. But I couldn't enter." Amanda watched as Rochele walked in place before her mother like she was trying to dance. And then the child looked at Amanda and she smiled. All the pale shadows Amanda had brought with her to Israel were suddenly banished. "I haven't held a baby since then."

Miriam studied her for a moment, then lifted her face and laughed. The sound was so surprising Rochele turned and giggled with her. Which only drew the old woman into louder glee.

The two ladies entered through the kitchen doorway and spoke to Miriam in Hebrew. The old woman answered in the same tongue. Whatever she said caused Alathea and the ladies to laugh as well.

Rochele positively loved the sound. She shouted her glee, a musical lilt that caused all the women to laugh harder still, including Amanda. When they quieted, Amanda asked, "What am I missing?"

"You know the prayer you carried for me to the Wall, yes?"

"It was about this child."

"So what happens, but the tourist from America who does me this kindness, who is she? A woman trained to help the sickest of babies. And then you come into my home. And this angel of my heart, this little one, she trusts you, and she comes to you."

"I was that nurse. No more."

Miriam waved that aside as if it were of no importance whatsoever. "You have come because the Holy One willed it. You will heal her."

Amanda protested, "If there was something detectable, the local doctors would have certainly found it by now."

This only caused Miriam to laugh louder. "What part of this miracle frightens you more? That you may be right? Or that you might be wrong?"

CHAPTER SIXTEEN

W hen the phone call came, Chris was so asleep he could not filter the jangling from his dream. He struggled up as from the depths driven by the fear that something was wrong and he was too far away to do anything about it. He knocked the clock to the floor before he found the phone and said, "Amanda?"

"No, it's me. Frank."

"What time is it?"

"I don't . . . Chris, can you come?"

Chris swung his feet to the floor. The drapes were drawn so he couldn't see across the street. The clock at his feet read just after two. "What's the matter?"

"I've fallen." Frank's voice sounded strangled. "It hurts, Chris. It hurts a lot."

The chief paramedic was named Chuck, and he was built like a professional wrestler, low to the ground and immensely strong. Which made his measured pace even more impressive. He told Frank, "Most likely you've cracked your hip joint, maybe even severed it entirely. So what we need to do is move you in slow stages, giving your muscles time to adjust to each new position. We're not going to pick you up, we're going to nudge your body slowly over so that it just flows as naturally as possible onto the gurney. Clear so far?"

"Sounds good," Frank said. His color had improved from the pasty complexion Chris had first seen. He'd located the house key where Frank said, under the potted bird of paradise beside the front stoop. He had found Frank halfway down the rear hall, where he had dragged himself in order to reach the hall phone.

Chuck went on, "Don't do anything, Frank. Don't move, don't try to help. Just put yourself totally in our hands. Can you do that?"

"Think so." Frank's tight panting breath had eased somewhat, but returned when the two EMTs took hold of his damaged side and slowly, slowly rolled him up a bit.

"Okay, here we go." While Chuck held Frank up, the silent young woman slid the stretcher underneath him. It was a narrow flat board with handles and a number of places where straps could be attached. Chuck tightened one strap across Frank's chest as soon as he was down flat again. "You still with me, Frank?"

"That hurt."

"Probably means your joint is a goner."

"I could feel something grind in there."

"We'll let the docs worry about that when we get you safe inside the ER. Now your upper body is stationary, so I'm going to nudge your legs slow and easy into position. Don't strain and don't try to help me. Ready?"

"Yes."

"Okay. Deep breath." Both attendants wore blue surgical gloves and handled Frank with an incredible mixture of strength and gentleness. Chris stood in the hall's far end and watched as the two attendants gradually pressed at Frank's good hip and thigh, nudging him slowly into position. Frank groaned once, then went back to panting.

"All done, Frank."

"That's it? Really?"

"We're good to go."

Frank released a huge breath. "Oh man."

Chris asked, "You want me to phone Emily?"

"No." Frank almost shouted the word. "You wait until I'm safe in the hospital and everything is under control. You hear me?"

"Sure thing," Chris said, using as soothing a tone as he could manage. "Whatever you say."

"I don't want her freaking out. And I need to be able to tell her I'm fine."

"Which you will be," Chuck said. "Okay, ready at your end? We lift on three. One, two, three."

When Frank was safely stowed in the back of the ambulance, Chuck said to Chris, "You're Amanda's husband, right?"

"Yes."

"Good to finally meet. Sorry it had to be like this." He locked the stretcher into place. "We've been praying for you."

"I'm sorry, what?"

"Yeah, we got this group at the hospital, we meet most mornings. Every time she's there, Amanda asks that we pray for you and the company. Avery, right? The electronics firm over past the airport?"

"Yes. I knew about the prayer group. But not about the prayers." From inside the ambulance he heard Frank chuckle. He looked through the door. "What's so funny?"

Frank waved a languid hand. "God's got you coming and going."

"Your wife is something else. I don't know what we would have done this year without her there to watch our backs." Chuck slammed the rear doors. "You going to follow us over?"

"Soon as I get on some clothes." He waved the ambulance away and discovered a pair of neighbors standing on their front step. He walked over in his beach sandals and pajama bottoms and explained what had happened, then hurried home to dress.

The driver's words rang in the silent night. No question about it. His wife was something else.

⟨∘⟩

Chris put off calling Emily as Frank had requested. He entered the hospital and was instantly surrounded by people who treated him with the down-to-earth calmness of old friends. The entire hospital staff seemed to know he was Amanda's husband and the friend of their beloved Frank. They knew why he was there, and they made him welcome. The hour did not matter a bit. There was none of the sitting around the vacant waiting room while they wheeled Frank up to radiology. They took Chris into the nurses' station and plied him with coffee they made fresh for him.

Chris knew most of them by name. He had been in and out of the hospital since before he and Amanda had married. But this was the first time he had been here with a need of his own, except of course for the disastrous night when Amanda had been forced into labor. And from some of the looks he received, sitting there in the comfortable chair sipping from the mug emblazoned with the hospital's logo, he suspected there were others who recalled that same night. When Amanda had woken in terrible pain and they had rushed over to learn that their baby's heart had stopped beating.

Chris found himself suddenly deluged by memories of that night, the urgency and the fear they had all shared, the tense speed that had surrounded their every action, their every breath. The sorrow and the helpless loss, and holding his wife after the birth while she cried herself to sleep. Amanda had been too worn out to give the tears much force. She had cried like a little girl. He had not recognized her voice. He had held her and worried that some fragment of their precious life together had been lost. And there was nothing he could do about it but hold her and cry tears of his own.

Chris found himself aching for his wife. Not for then. For now. What it must mean for her to come through those doors and face those memories every day. How much she must love this place. It was not a job. It was not a place filled with sickness and injury and fear. It was her calling. And not even desperate loss would keep her away.

He was so proud of her he could have wept.

"Chris?"

"Dr. Henri. How are you?"

"I should be asking you that." The man's skin shone softly in the fluorescents. He wore his customary surgical blues and stern expression.

"I was thinking of the night. You know, when—"

"I suspected as much. Do you want to talk about it?"

"No," he decided. "There really isn't anything to be said. It happened. We're dealing with it."

Dr. Henri walked to the coffeemaker in the corner and poured himself a mug full. "It's a shame that life does not give us a time free of other worries when we can heal."

Chris huffed a humorless laugh. "You can say that again."

Dr. Henri settled into the chair across from Chris. "I suppose you have family who think you should have left it all behind by now."

"Yes, actually we do."

"Among my people, we talk about the cycles of life. That grief has its own season. And being impatient for it to pass is as futile as arguing with winter."

"Your people sound very wise," Chris said.

"About some things, perhaps." Dr. Henri gestured toward the door. "We have a prayer meeting that starts in twenty minutes. Would you like to join me?"

Chris looked at his watch. "It's ten past six."

"That is correct."

"I've been sitting here for almost three hours."

"You have indeed."

"Do you have any news about Frank?"

"The surgeon has arrived. Frank is being prepped. They are going to replace the joint."

"I need to call Emily."

"You could," Dr. Henri solemnly agreed. "But she is in Israel, is she not? With your own good wife, I believe."

"Yes."

"So is there an urgency in calling and making her worry? In three more hours Frank will be out of surgery, and you can call her with the good news."

"If it were me, I'd want to know now."

"You might. Then again, you would suffer through three hours of frantically trying to get back home, worrying over things out of your control."

The man had a straightforward way of puncturing Chris's logic. "Maybe I should wait."

"I would advise it."

"If I catch it for not telling her sooner, I'm going to blame it on you."

Dr. Henri might have smiled. It was hard to tell. "It would not be the first time."

∾

The hospital's large public cafeteria had a smaller room off to one side. And off this was yet a smaller room, where all the tables were clustered together and clearly intended as a sort of informal conference area. They filled all the chairs around the table and drew in more so that people lined the side and rear wall. Chris was given a place of honor at the front with Dr. Henri. To his right was a glass wall overlooking a narrow strip of green and medical office buildings beyond. A number of people came over and said hello. Their concern and warmth were both touching and a little surprising. They all knew about his company's troubles and appeared genuinely concerned about his own well-being.

Dr. Henri led them in an opening prayer, asking for Frank's

peace and healing, and then prayed for Emily. Then he prayed for Amanda on her journey and for Chris and for the company. He spoke of them with such an easy familiarity that Chris knew this was far from the first time he had made such requests. There was no reason why he should be so moved by the simple words. He knew Amanda was greatly loved here.

When Dr. Henri went silent, one voice after another spoke briefly, encircling the room with reflective harmony. Chris sat with his eyes open and his heart full. The light was strong now, another beautiful December day in Florida. Chris stared out the window and wondered at how many lovely dawns he had been blind to over the past months. A cluster of gulls swooped past, and he felt his own heart take wing.

CHAPTER SEVENTEEN

Amanda arrived back at the hotel filled with genuine misgivings. Her concerns had not truly surfaced until she was on the bus and headed toward Jerusalem, but they continued to mount until she felt that every voice surrounding her as she passed through the bus terminal was accusing her of arrogance. How could she, a stranger to this land and these people, hope to discover what ailed this child? She had two days. The doctors had been working on her for two years. The miracle that Miriam had spoken of was nothing but a mockery. A false hope. Amanda wasn't even a nurse anymore.

She felt like the sun was trying to beat her into the pavement. Her footsteps grew increasingly heavy as she walked the mile back to the hotel. Climbing the front steps required a huge effort. She endured the security check and entered the hotel's cool air-conditioned wash. She was almost to the elevators when she realized the desk clerk was calling her name.

Amanda walked back over and was greeted by smiles from

all the staff. Even the manager appeared in the doorway to her office and watched as the senior clerk reached behind and lifted a vase of roses from the table holding guests' mail. "We will be sorry to have these go upstairs with you."

Amanda made no move to take them. "There must be some mistake."

"A secret admirer," the manager almost sang the words. "There, see the card? It came with the flowers."

Her hands shook slightly as she opened the tiny envelope, pulled out the card, and read *For my darling, thank you for the gift of your love. Chris.*

Amanda said numbly, "They're from my husband."

"Ah, now you have spoiled my day," the manager said, pretending to be upset. "I will go home and there will be no flowers waiting for me, no sweet note. Like every day. Only this evening, I will miss them."

"You are married to a saint of a man," the desk clerk told the manager. "I should be so lucky as to find a man like yours."

"Did I say otherwise? No, I did not." The manager was stout and gray-haired and smiled at the flowers. "But roses would make for such a sweet hello, yes?"

Amanda tucked the card into her pocket and carried the vase with both hands. She caught sight of her goofy smile in the elevator's mirror. The surprise had come at the perfect moment. She could not even remember what she had been so worried about.

❧

Amanda showered and lay down on her bed and fell asleep looking at the flowers. She awoke when Emily slipped the key into the door and opened her eyes to the sunset turning their room golden. A languid ease filled her. She stared at the pale blue sky beyond their window, content to do nothing but enjoy the smooth flow of her own breathing. She had not known such a moment since the days of her pregnancy. Back then she had often stopped and rested, claiming it was what the doctor ordered, but in truth doing so because she wanted to revel in the life that was growing inside her. A part of her, and yet totally unique. She had never felt so complete as in those moments. It was a revelation, something utterly unexpected and yet so incredibly natural. Chris had bought a rocking chair for the nursery and placed it across from the crib and close to the rear window. Amanda had loved to sit and listen to the soft creaking and caress her growing tummy.

Emily emerged from the bathroom. "Where did the roses come from?"

"Chris sent them."

"What a wonderful man." Emily stretched out on her bed. "They're lovely."

"I was so worried when I got back, and then here they were."

"Worried about the child?"

"Yes. Her name is Rochele." Amanda sat up and told Emily about the girl.

"Maybe that's why you went. So you could hold a child again. Be a nurse. Care for someone."

Amanda reached out and touched one of the flowers. "Maybe." She turned and looked at her friend in the next bed. "I'm sorry."

"For what?"

"For keeping you at arm's length all last year. For not getting to know you before now."

Emily looked at her. "First of all, there's no need to apologize. You did what you needed to do. Second, you need to recognize that a change has come. I know because I've been through it. You are rejoining with life. There may be moments when you feel overwhelmed by guilt or sorrow or just a nameless dread. I want you to remember this, being here with me, and I want you to tell me you're ready to get on with whatever comes next. That you're ready to *hope* again."

Amanda tasted a smile. "I am."

"Good girl." Emily swung her feet to the floor. "Then let's get dressed and eat. I'm starving."

↷

When the phone rang, Amanda was in the bathroom putting on her makeup. She waited to see if Emily called her in, then remained where she was, granting her friend a bit of privacy. When the voice went silent, Amanda opened the bathroom door to find Emily seated in their room's only chair. The older woman stared out the window, her face streaked by tears. She cradled the phone against her chest with both hands as though it were a child.

"What's the matter?"

Emily blinked twice, dislodging another tear. "I have to go home."

All of Amanda's protests were stifled by the expression on her friend's face. Emily showed no sorrow, nor worry. Instead, she wore a look of gentle astonishment. Amanda walked over and seated herself on the side of the bed. "Tell me what's happened."

"Frank fell. He's in the hospital."

The professionally trained component of her mind slipped into gear. Amanda could almost feel the wheels grind. "Emily, look at me. Give me the long version, please."

"It happened last night. Frank heard something pop in his hip and he fell. He said the pain was ferocious."

Amanda examined her friend, unsettled by the eerie calm. And yet there were no telltale signs of shock. "This probably means the joint gave way. It happens. They'll get him settled, do a scan, then start on the replacement procedure—"

"Oh, I know all that. It's already happened."

"He had his surgery?"

"He's back in his room."

"Emily, are you all right?"

"Me? I've never been better." And she smiled. "Why do you ask?"

"You look, well . . . happy."

"I'm more than that. I'm positively awestruck." Emily reached over and took her hand. "Do you know what just happened?"

"I have absolutely no idea."

"The answer to my prayer. The reason I came to Israel."

"You were afraid about Frank's response to needing surgery?"

"Of course not. I'm talking about our daughter."

"You could not have lost me more if I were in a different hotel."

Emily's smile broke out once more. "No, I suppose I'm making a mess of explaining."

"Stop talking in riddles and tell me!"

"Frank wants us to reconnect with Lucy."

Amanda rocked back. "What?"

The tears started flowing again. Emily gave no sign she noticed. "Frank prayed that God would give him a sign. Something to show that a change really had taken place. That the bad times really were behind us."

When Emily stopped, Amanda thumped their joined hands on her leg. "Tell me what happened."

"Frank spent all of ninety seconds telling me about his fall and the surgery. Then he just flicked away my questions and started in on Lucy. While they were together, Lucy told Frank she wanted to name her daughter after the baby girl we lost."

Amanda felt her own vision blur. "Emily, that's . . ."

"Lucy said she could not make up for the lost years. Or the pain she'd caused us. But she wanted to do what she could to replace what had been taken from us."

CHAPTER EIGHTEEN

C hris answered Amanda's call just as he was leaving
Frank's room. She was speaking from the hotel lobby
and using what Chris called her hospital voice, crisp
and precise and professional. Even so, when she thanked him
for the flowers, her voice turned to honey. She gave him Emily's
flight details, then asked if he minded her staying for the two
remaining days and leaving when planned. Chris replied that
he had assumed this was what she had planned to do all along,
which seemed to relieve her and trouble her in equal measure.
When he asked if anything was the matter, she cupped the
phone and told him about a little girl named Rochele. Chris felt
himself growing numb as he listened, assured her it was fine that
she stayed, shut his phone, started the car, and left the hospital's
multi-deck parking lot.

He drove home, traveling against the grim-faced flow of
people headed for the industrial parks and the jobs they hoped
they would still have next week. But he wouldn't think about

that now. Frank was well, the man's conversation with Emily had apparently gone great, and Amanda was off again tomorrow treating a sick baby . . .

Chris walked around his front yard, thinking about a world six thousand miles away and how it impacted them here at home. Amanda had told him about her attempted foray into the maternity ward and how it had ended with her fleeing in a panic. Yet now here she was doing what came naturally. Helping the helpless. Caring for the little ones. Giving them a chance at a whole tomorrow.

He knew what was troubling her. She doubted whether she could actually help the baby get well. He knew he should be caring more about the child's illness. But just then all he could think of was how amazing it was to hear that resolve in her voice. His wife, the critical care nurse.

He locked the car, went inside, changed into his jogging shorts, and carried his smile out for a run.

When he returned an hour later, he stretched in the back-yard, then carried the good feeling inside, picking up the clothes he had scattered in his hasty departure that morning. He showered and dressed, planning to go back to the hospital. Then he decided to lie down on the bed, thinking he would rest just a few minutes. But he shut his eyes and was gone.

In his dream he stared into the face of his wife and heard her speak his name. "Christopher."

The soft music of that one word propelled him from sleep. It carried him out of the bed and across the bedroom and out the back door into the closing light of day.

The back of their yard was lined by bamboo, forming a golden hedge in the sunset, rising up twenty-five feet in places.

When the wind came off the ocean, like now, the cane rustled and sighed, as musical as living chimes.

Chris stood by the screen and rubbed the sleep from his face. Amanda's soft voice called his name once more. "Christopher". It was a vivid memory now, strong as the salt on the ocean breeze.

Most of the time she called him by the name the rest of the world used. Chris. He liked it well enough. He knew some families where the longer version of a name was something that only emerged in anger. Amanda never did that.

Christopher was the name she spoke in their special moments, turning it into a secret melody, one she sang only for him. That one word always carried a wealth of feeling, so much that it seemed like a language all their own. The light in her eyes was so clear, her love so potent, she humbled him. She saw to the very heart of him, through all the fears and pains and misgivings and failures. And she loved him. She gave herself to him fully. Those were the most beautiful and complete moments he had ever known. And far more than he had ever deserved.

Only when the sky went dark and he returned inside did he realize his face was wet.

∽

After breakfast the next morning, Amanda left Emily to finish packing. She walked through the hotel lobby and entered the morning sunlight. The air was cool in a manner very different from Florida. There was no humidity, which meant the chill was deceptive. When she was in the sunlight, it was possible to ignore just how cold the air remained. Even this early the light was brilliant and powerful. She greeted the two guards who were on permanent duty outside the hotel, one to check cars and the other to inspect all baggage and people before permitting them entry. She walked around the side of the building and entered the small city park. This time of morning, many of the benches were filled with locals reading from tiny black books, men and women alike, seated where they could see the Old City and perform their morning prayers. There was a quiet intensity to the place, a feeling that all who came were offered a moment apart from the world and its woes. It was a good place to call Chris and ask permission to do the impossible.

She was a little nervous. It was hard to identify precisely what caused her stomach to ripple with apprehension. As she dialed the number for their home, Amanda decided it was simply a desire not to quarrel. Even so, she needed to explain fully what was going on here, and how grave her concerns were. What she wanted most of all from Chris was his blessing.

Chris answered with the deep voice that told her she'd woken him up. "I know it's the middle of the night, but this can't wait. I'm taking Emily to the airport and then going back to see this little girl. And I'm scared, Chris. I need to talk this through with you. I need you to tell me what to do."

He was quiet a long moment, then said, "All right, Amanda. I'm listening."

The need to get through this was so strong her words came in a rush. "Emily has to go back. But she's ready because her miracle has happened. I know that sounds ridiculous, but it's the truth. She didn't come to see Israel. She came to pray for a miracle and it's happened."

He sounded much more awake now. "You're talking about Frank and Lucy."

"Yes. I've prayed for my own miracle, and I need to stay and see it through."

He sounded almost detached as he responded, "What is your miracle, Amanda?"

"I told you about the child. Rochele is such a lovely baby. She's sick and the doctors won't help her. I don't know what I can do. I have no access to her records. But I feel like it's important . . . No, that's not correct. I *know* it's important for me to stay. It's *vital*, Chris. I need to try and help this little girl heal. And at the same time, it sounds crazy, just hearing myself say those words. What on earth can I possibly do with my few hours here that the doctors haven't done themselves?"

There was no hesitation. No emotion, really. Just this deep resonance that carried an exceptional sense of certainty. "That's not the miracle, Amanda."

"What?"

"You're not asking for the miracle you need. You're talking about the child. But that's not about *you*."

She turned and walked farther along the path to where she could step off the cobblestones and enter into a clump of desert pines. The air was spiced with their scent.

Chris asked, "Are you still there?"

"Yes. I'm thinking about what you said." The needles were laced with sunlight and formed a veil through which she could see the golden wall of Jerusalem. "You're right."

Chris remained silent.

"I didn't come here to ask for a child to heal. I asked for *me* to heal."

"And us."

The two simple words released a dam of emotions. She had

not even realized she was holding back, she had repressed them for so long. But suddenly, here in the tiny enclave fashioned from the same ancient trees that shaded the park by the tomb, Amanda found herself weeping. "Just a minute."

She searched her purse for a tissue. She wiped her eyes and glanced around, shamed by her public spectacle. She could see two people seated in their own private spaces on a pair of benches. Neither of them seemed aware of her.

"Talk to me, Amanda."

"When I wrote the prayer and placed it in the Wailing Wall, I prayed for a healing. I didn't know what exactly that meant until now."

Chris was the one who went quiet. Finally he said, "Will you do something for me?"

"Anything," she replied, and meant it with all her heart.

"I want you to write another prayer and put it in the Wall. For me. For us."

"I didn't bring a pen with me."

"I think you'll remember. Write this." His voice crumpled momentarily. He coughed, took a pair of puffing breaths, and said, "O Lord our God, restore the heart and the joy of our marriage. Amen."

CHAPTER NINETEEN

Amanda saw Emily off at the airport and waved her through the security checkpoint. She did not stop waving until the older woman had passed through customs. On the bus down from Jerusalem, Amanda had feared she would become swamped with lonely feelings of vulnerability. But it was not like that at all. Instead, she felt a sober certainty that she was doing the right thing, no matter how wildly bizarre it might appear to someone else. Once back in Jerusalem, she returned to the bus station and found someone willing to take her by the hand and lead her to the bus headed to Bet Jola. The locals' brusqueness did not disturb her at all. She settled into the day's third bus and found herself looking forward to seeing Rochele again.

Then it hit her.

Amanda cried aloud, "She has jaundice!"

The woman seated next to her was so stout she spilled over the seat and pressed tight against Amanda. The woman swiveled as much as the bus's confines permitted and squinted at her. Amanda could not help exclaiming, "The baby is jaundiced. I should have realized it instantly. But it's been so long since I've seen a jaundiced baby, I didn't even think of it."

Another woman leaned toward her from across the aisle and spoke in English, "You are having a problem?"

"I was. I did. Yesterday I was asked to look at a baby who has been ill since birth." Amanda wanted to sing, shout her joy to the sky. "But I didn't even realize what I was looking at until now."

The woman translated swiftly. The bus was filled to the brim, all seats taken and four soldiers sitting on their packs in the central aisle. Every face was watching them now as the woman asked, "You are a doctor?"

"A maternity nurse. I specialize in crisis care."

This, too, was translated. "So you are able to see what the Israeli doctors have not?"

"I don't know. Maybe. And that's the point."

"Please?"

"I started by asking the wrong questions. Which is what they did. Maybe. It's just hit me now. I need to start by assuming everything has been done absolutely right. And if this is true, then what could be logically overlooked?"

Heads up and down the bus were watching them as the woman translated. "Jaundice is not such a rare thing."

"Jaundice is not the problem. It's just another symptom. And this child has so many. The doctors probably thought the jaundice was the result of an autoimmune disease, which is what I assumed the girl has."

"How old is she, this girl?"

"Two years."

"She has been sick long?"

"Since birth."

As soon as the woman across the aisle had translated, the other passengers moaned a soft chorus. Even the bus driver was watching her now through the rearview mirror. "Where does she live?"

"Bet Jola."

This resulted in a rapid discussion that was carried along by a dozen voices, including that of the stout woman seated next to her. The self-appointed translator said, "This child's parents, they are immigrants?"

"From Tunisia. The father has died. The mother works as a cleaner."

The woman sniffed her way through the translation. This time the bus driver waved his hand to punctuate his angry tirade. The woman said, "The doctors who treat this child will be working for a free clinic. They will be very tired. Very . . . what is the word?"

"Stressed. Overworked. Carrying enormous caseloads."

"Impatient, yes. So they see this child over and over, and now they dismiss the woman. They tell her with their faces and their manner, this child, she is going to die."

"That is *not* going to happen."

The woman was clearly very pleased with Amanda's response. "You are certain you know what is wrong with this little one?"

"No, of course not." Amanda hesitated, then added, "But I would bet money I'm right. If I were a betting person. Which I'm not."

The woman's translation resulted in another tirade by the driver, followed by three others. The stout woman beside her became so upset she bounced in her seat with each word, vibrating against Amanda.

"How did you meet this child?" asked the woman across the aisle.

"It's a long story."

She sniffed again. "And what else are we to do with our time on this bus than hear about the sick child?"

So Amanda told the story. About visiting the Wailing Wall with her friend. About seeing the young rabbis accost others. About the stranger who offered to guide them inside.

The bus made a stop. No one left, but two teens climbed aboard, chattering gaily. The driver and two old men seated up near the front sharply rebuked them. The teens subsided into startled silence. The doors squeaked shut and the bus trundled on.

Amanda described how Miriam asked her to write out the prayer and set it into the Wall. She told about taking this same bus to the village yesterday, and going to the house, and spending the afternoon with the little girl.

Her words were greeted with a moment's silence and then the bus driver spoke. A bearded old man seated up front chimed an agreement. The woman translated, "There is a saying in our tongue. It speaks of the special place in heaven reserved for the righteous Gentile. We are certain you are counted among them."

The bus rolled to a halt.

"This is your stop, yes?" The woman across the aisle rose from her seat. "Come. We go together."

"My name, it is Nechama. In Hebrew this means comfort." She rolled her eyes at her own statement, as though telling Amanda a joke. She exited the bus behind Amanda and demanded, "Which way do we go?"

Nechama had the face of a fighter, with fierce eyes and a chin that was ready to jut forward at a moment's notice. Amanda had the distinct impression that the woman was ready for any protest she might put forth.

Nechama set a briskly impatient pace. At the last turning, Amanda did not recognize any of the buildings. But just as she was ready to confess she had led them down a wrong street, the little house with its ratty front garden came into view.

Miriam had been waiting for her because the door opened as Amanda pushed through the front gate. When Amanda introduced her companion, the two women instantly launched into a lengthy discussion in Hebrew, which continued as Miriam led them through the house and into the same back bedroom.

Rochele was alone. As Miriam lifted her up, the child gave the stranger a solemn inspection, then reached out for Amanda to take her.

Miriam smiled as she released the little one. "She is glad you came."

Amanda carried Rochele back into the living room where the cook emerged long enough to welcome Nechama and then again to bring them tea. Amanda felt a comfortable sense of belonging as the conversation in Hebrew swirled around her. The cook emerged from the kitchen to join in and the conversation grew increasingly voluble. The cook waved her arms and dabbed at the corner of her eyes with her apron. The tirade was loud enough to draw the helper in from the back garden, and she added her own volume to the discussion.

Nechama's voice and expression grew ever more severe. Finally she clattered her glass into the little saucer, rose to her feet, and spoke her first words of English since entering the home. "I have heard enough. Let us go and speak with these doctors."

❧

Miriam set a surprisingly swift pace for a woman supported by a cane. They were midway down the lane leading to Bet Jola's central thoroughfare when they met Rochele's mother coming toward them. Alathea heard their plans with rising anxiety, her face going pale with worry over confronting the doctors. But when she started protesting, Nechama cut her off with such intensity the woman meekly fell into step beside Amanda.

Miriam directed them into the central market. Here and there were vestiges of the original village, now almost swamped by wave after wave of poor immigrants seeking work in the factories and offices rimming Jerusalem. The market was filled with second-rate produce and noise.

Amanda reached over and took Rochele from the fretful mother. The little girl's face shone with a delight that bordered on wonder. Amanda turned this way and that, allowing Rochele to stare at a stall selling live songbirds hung in wicker cages. Then came the spices, great rainbow mounds of colors and scents. The air was cramped with diesel and cooking lamb and coriander and mint. Amanda slowed a bit, as much for herself as the child. She turned with Rochele, reveling in the gift of seeing the world through young eyes.

When they finally emerged from the market, Amanda hurried to catch up with the others. She wondered if there was some way to do what Chris had prayed. Because that really was what lay behind his words. To be restored meant returning to what had been lost. Amanda always said that such things as love and joy had to come naturally. And yet here she was, feeling a shared sense of hope in the impossible happening. A return to what had always been so simple, until it was lost. She had spent an entire year running from the hollowness at the center of her world. She ached for the one who should have been there in her arms. And now, as she walked the road with strangers, carrying a child who was not her own, Amanda found herself feeling threatened. As though part of her feared growing beyond where she was and allowing herself to be happy again.

She was still mulling this over as they rounded a corner and the town's clinic came into view. As soon as Rochele saw their destination, she whimpered and reached for her mother. Amanda relinquished the child, and their little group walked past the men standing in the shadows cast by the tall buildings to either side, filling the outer passage with their cigarette smoke.

As they entered the clinic, Amanda faced a new realization about herself. The difference between this moment and the life she had known before the crisis came down to one simple fact: she now knew with raw vividness that her world could be turned upside down. It was indeed possible for her happiness to be stripped away. If she allowed herself to be happy, she had to learn to live with the risk that she might someday lose it once more.

And beneath it all, hidden in the dark shadows of a sorrow she had struggled to release and yet clenched tightly to her soul, was yet another truth. She was terrified of becoming pregnant again. Not of losing the little one. Of *everything*. The risks involved loomed about her on all sides.

Somewhere in the distance an infant wailed and Amanda shivered with genuine terror. That could so easily be her own baby in pain. If she let herself have a next time.

Miriam stepped up beside her and asked softly, "Do you want to speak of it?"

Amanda started as though she had been jerked awake. "Excuse me?"

"Come, child. You will sit with me. No, no, not here. We have no appointment and no emergency. The doctors do not want to see us, so they will punish us for coming by taking our time. It is the way."

Miriam led her back outside. The clinic opened onto a stubby road, too broad to be called an alley, and barred at the end so that only two ancient ambulances were parked along its length. The result was a sort of plaza for the clinic's visitors. Benches lined both sides. Those within the shade cast by the building to their left were all taken. A pair of men, swarthy and with the biggest moustaches Amanda had ever seen, rose and waved them over. The gesture was very Mediterranean, the underhanded sweep, the half bow toward the older woman. They spoke in halting Hebrew and gestured again, both of them as polite as courtiers.

Miriam thanked them with the ease of one who was long accustomed to such treatment and asked Amanda, "Do you mind sitting in the sunlight?"

"Not at all."

"We will find it more private." Only when they were seated themselves did the men return to their bench and their quiet conversation. "Back on the road, you grew so very sad."

Amanda knew it was an invitation to speak. She knew also that if she did not respond, Miriam would not press. It was very strange, this level of understanding with a woman who was so totally a stranger. They had nothing in common, and yet they shared a bond forged while standing before a wall from beyond the reach of time. Amanda said, "I'm so afraid."

Miriam folded her hands in her lap and waited.

Amanda started with the conversation with Chris that morning and worked backward, then returned to the present. And her fears.

When she went silent, Miriam waited a time, making sure she was done. Then she said, "Do you know what is nice? You do not need to ask me why I am not with my sons. In America. So beautiful, there. And they are rich. And they tell me to come. Every time they phone, they beg and they plead. Come. Live here. You have a room, a place that is yours. Why you are staying there all alone? Why you do not live with us, your family? On and on the questions and the quarreling."

The clinic doors opened, emitting a cloud of astringent odors. Amanda only noticed them now, when she was outside in the sunlight. It was often that way back home. After a day on the wards she only smelled the difference when she stepped outside and breathed air that was not clogged with hospital smells. Through the open doorway she could see Nechama standing by the counter, arguing with the receptionist. Alathea stood beside her, with Rochele using her mother's hair as a veil to hide behind.

Miriam went on, "I do not tell them the reasons, because my sons would not understand, and the truth would hurt them. So I remain silent and I wait for them to stop with their arguments. But here is the truth, the reason I remain in Bet Jola." The old woman turned so as to face Amanda full on. "Because I was born to be a mother. Do you understand what I say?"

"I'm not . . . I don't . . ."

"My one son, the doctor in Chicago, he has married a lovely American woman from a good family. She does not like me. She tries hard to hide this truth. But how could I not know? She has a woman from Ecuador who lives in their house and cares for the children. She is afraid that I will come and try to take this woman's place. She thinks I am old-fashioned. She thinks I will make the children not fit in her modern world." Miriam stared over Amanda's shoulder, the rheumy eyes studying the unseen. She shrugged. "*Nu*, who is to say, perhaps she is correct in her thinking."

Amanda asked gently, "And your other son?"

"Ah, the other. Such a gentle spirit. Such a lovely boy. He lives in San Francisco. With his partner." She drew out that last word. "You understand?"

"I do."

"For this and only this I am glad my beloved husband rests with the angels." Miriam dismissed it with a wave of one arthritic hand. "I was born in that house. I raised my children there. I watched them grow and I watched them leave. And I lost my husband. All the hollow emptiness. And I prayed for an answer, even though I did not know the question to ask. You understand what I am saying, yes?"

Amanda nodded. "All too well."

"I watched the little village I knew as a child become swallowed by a new Israel. Emigrant Jews from places I had never heard of, Ethiopia and Casablanca and Tunis and Alexandria and Sana. Remnants of the Diaspora, all coming home to a land they had never known. Their children, they are lost and frightened and need a haven. First I take in one child. Neighbors who work long hours, husband and wife both. They bring another family. And this family brings a third. And suddenly I have thirty-two children, and two helpers, and a home that is filled with life. And here now is the wonder. My arms and my heart. They are no longer empty."

Miriam's fingers did not quite straighten. The joints kept them slightly curled, even as she reached over and poked Amanda's leg. "Why am I telling you this? Because I understand your fears. I have walked a different path and arrived at the same place. And here is the answer, the *only* answer I have found. If you are open, the Almighty will find a way. But only if you are open."

The clinic doors creaked once again, and Nechama called to them, "The doctor will see us now."

CHAPTER TWENTY

But of course the doctor did not see them. Their turn had simply come to shift from the waiting area to one of the inspection rooms. The cubicles were open-fronted, with thick drapes hanging from metal poles. The rings rattled each time drapes were opened and shut. Amanda saw Rochele jerk with fear each time the sound came in from somewhere down the long concrete corridor. The smells were pungent, the noise unsettling for everyone but Amanda. Nechama clearly disliked being shuffled along a medical assembly line. She spoke in an angry hiss to Miriam, clearly trying to tone down her outrage so as to not spook the child further. But Amanda knew there was nothing to be gained from pressing. She tried to divert Nechama's attention with a question. "What is it you do?"

"Do? Do?"

"I mean, professionally."

"I am, how you say . . ." Nechama spoke to Miriam in Hebrew. Miriam shrugged in reply.

A deep male voice from beyond the curtains said, "She is an office manager."

"Thank you," Amanda said. There was no response.

"No, no, is not correct. I do not just manage. I *maintain*. Five lawyers and three secretaries and eleven aides. They are . . . *mishugga*."

This word Amanda had heard enough to be able to translate herself. "Crazy."

"Yes. Like this medical system. A mess. A wreck. To make a baby wait like this, how is it possible?"

"It's fine," Amanda said. "How can you take time to help us?"

"Because I am also a mother," Nechama replied heatedly. "A mother who knows how this system works. Or *fails* to work. That is why."

"It is very good of you both to come," Miriam said. "For you both to help us as you do."

"Yes, of course, Grandmother speaks the truth. I help because you, the tourist, take time from your holiday. To do what?" Nechama raised her voice. "To stand in this place and wait all day for a doctor who does not come!"

Before Amanda could respond, the drapes swept back. The deep male voice they had heard before said, "*Nu*, observe. A miracle. The doctor, he is here."

Nechama's retort was stifled by the ringing of her phone. She pulled it from her jacket pocket and sniffed. "One of the crazies needs me."

The doctor was surprisingly slight for the depth of his voice. He had the slender build of a violinist. She suspected that he was only a few years older than she, but weariness and strain had aged him.

Rochele scrunched herself up tightly to her mother's neck, refusing to even look the doctor's way. He grimaced at the sound of the child's whimper and touched the place where soft hairs met the nape of her neck. She whimpered once more.

He softly greeted the two other women, then said to Amanda, "This child, I am knowing. Her mother, I am knowing. And Miss Miriam, guardian of many young lives, I am knowing her as well. You, I am not knowing."

"My name is Amanda Vance."

"And why are you here?"

"I was wondering, well . . ." Amanda hesitated. She had no idea how to proceed. "I am a nurse."

The man shrugged his unconcern and rubbed tired eyes. "Nurses we have."

"I wanted to ask if you would please check the child's medical records."

"Of course we have records. What, you think because you are in Israel you will find no records?"

"I mean no disrespect."

"You are suggesting that you can come and question my work here, this means no insult?" He crossed his arms. "How is this possible? Please tell me."

Before Amanda could respond, the doctor sighed, flipped back the drapes, and stepped outside. The curtain blocking out the corridor had been washed until the original color was lost. The doctor returned, causing Rochele to flinch once more as he swept the curtains shut. He carried a manila folder so crammed with pages it had accordioned out to a full eight inches thick. The file represented a tragic history of treatments and tests and specialists and discussions. For a little girl just two years old.

The doctor must have seen something in her face, for his irritated tone diminished somewhat. "*Nu.* The file. Now ask your question."

"Has Rochele ever been treated with sulfa drugs? And if so, what was the response?"

The doctor cocked his head. "The symptoms have been with her since birth or soon after."

"I understand."

"They were not caused by our treatment."

"I am not asking in regard to the origins of her illness. I am looking for the patient's response to one specific issue."

"A symptom."

"Actually, a causal link."

The doctor used both hands to settle the file on the examining table and started leafing through the pages. "I am sure we have tried the sulfas. We have tried everything when the fevers strike. You know about the fevers?"

Amanda nodded. She watched him turn page after page. Hoping.

"Yes. Here. We tried. Eight months ago."

"Her response?"

"We thought we had lost her. I remember the night. I was not here, but I heard the next day. The fever spiked so high she entered spasms. They put her on IV and ice bath. Constant supervision for eighteen hours. Then it vanished."

Amanda felt a soft humming race through her body, a faint trill of hope. "Has her blood work suggested a fairly constant jaundice?"

The doctor squinted at her. "You know the answer."

Amanda nodded as Nechama returned to stand beside Miriam. "I think so. Yes."

"So tell me what says the file."

"Severe anemia is one of the outcomes of every fever. You treat the jaundice with blood strengtheners. They help. But if you keep her on them, they seem to make other symptoms worse."

He looked at her a long moment. Turned the pages. Nodded more to himself than to her. But it was enough to cause Amanda's tremors to strengthen.

"There is more to your question, yes?"

"Just two more parts. Is she allergic to chickpeas?"

"To . . ." He turned and spoke to the mother. Alathea gave Amanda a look of wide-eyed wonder and spoke what was such a clear affirmative the doctor did not even translate. Even Nechama's fierce readiness to do battle was shaken.

Amanda heard the tremors echo now in her voice. "Has her blood work ever included a full enzyme test?"

"Why would we be following such a very expensive protocol?"

"Sometimes a pattern of jaundice suggests a causal link to enzymes."

"Very rare." Even so, the doctor was nodding. "All right. Tell me."

She could tell the doctor knew what she was going to say. But she said it anyway. "G-6PD."

"Impossible," the doctor said instantly. "This you are also already knowing."

Nechama broke in with, "What is this you have said?"

"Glucose-6-phosphate dehydrogenase deficiency," Amanda

answered, giving the full medical name. "It's a hereditary ailment characterized by abnormally low levels of a specific enzyme."

"It is also exclusively a *male* illness," the doctor said. Even so, his hostility was utterly gone. He addressed Amanda as he would any other professional. "And as we both know, Rochele is most definitely a female."

Amanda lifted her hand, halting Nechama while the office manager was still drawing in her breath. "Actually, there has recently been a change to this perception. Last year scientists made a definite tie between the illness and a defect in the male chromosome."

The doctor crossed his arms, but not in defense. He adopted the tight tone of a man on a quest. "You are sure of this how? I ask because, as we both know, all patients who suffer from G-6PD are from this part of the world. It is not a disease of the Americas. Caucasians do not suffer this enzyme deficiency."

"In my hospital in Florida, we almost lost a little girl. One of my last cases. She was in and out of intensive care for the first eighteen months of her life. Her father was Lebanese." The recollections were so intense and vivid they brought tears to Amanda's eyes. "She was brought in with a fever that terrified us. As we were fitting the IV she went into spasms so tight we feared she might snap a vertebra. We raced to the ice machine, scooping out handfuls and filling the space around her. We already knew she had an allergy to most analgesics; we couldn't even administer paracetamol. The mother was held in the corner by an aide and kept screaming for us to do something. I've never felt more helpless in my life. But a doctor on our staff had an idea."

The doctor was nodding with his entire body, rocking so

that his thighs came in contact with the examining table. "And what did this doctor say?"

"His name is Henri Beausejour. Dr. Henri is from the Dominican Republic, but his heritage is African. And as you know, G-6PD is the most common hereditary disease in West Africa. He told us of a UN study completed just months before. It proved incontrovertibly a direct link to the male chromosome. And just as male chromosomes are latent in some females, the disease in infant girls almost always remains dormant. Most female carriers of this deficiency will have it their entire lives, and perhaps think they have severe allergic reactions to sulfas or fava beans. Only when the father was a sufferer was the disease shown to become an active threat in daughters."

The doctor continued rocking. "And you knew that Rochele's father passed early."

"From respiratory complications. Which are also a symptom of G-6PD. Yes. Miriam told me."

"Your patient, the little Lebanese girl, how is she?"

"I don't . . . I have not heard."

"You are no longer a nurse?"

Amanda wiped her cheeks. "Not for over a year."

The doctor took his time settling the pages in the file back into place. "I am thinking this is a very great shame."

❧

The doctor's name was Korban. He asked them all to wait, excused himself, departed, then returned and sheepishly apologized for not having introduced himself. The change in his attitude was so total, Nechama actually felt comfortable saying,

"I must leave. There is another urgent matter. Probably one of my lawyers has forgotten where he left his *yarmulke*."

"I cannot thank you enough for making this happen," Amanda said.

"What have I done? Nothing, is what. You are the miracle worker." Nechama waved off Amanda's protests. "And now you will come and join us for dinner, yes? You can take a taxi from your hotel. Here is my card. Here, the number for my cell phone, which is surgically attached. Here the address of our home in Hebrew. Show this to the taxi driver. Tell him if he charges you the tourist price he will answer to me. Seven o'clock, it is not too late? Good-bye."

The cubicle seemed to expand somewhat, as though air rushed in to fill the vacuum left by Nechama's departure. Miriam spoke with Alathea in Hebrew, then said to Amanda, "I should go."

"Of course."

"My assistants, they are good-hearted, and the children love them. But they need a firm hand." She embraced Amanda with the ease of long friends taking leave. "What Nechama says, it is true. This is a day of miracles."

"I'm glad I could help. Perhaps. We won't know for certain until—"

"Please. Let an old woman feel the joy of knowing, without doubt, yes? Will I see you again?"

Amanda realized with a start that her work here was done. Either the tests revealed what she suspected and the little one responded to the treatments, or not. Either way she had nothing left to offer. Yet she loathed the idea of saying good-bye to Miriam. "Can you come back to Jerusalem tomorrow? I need to go back to the Wall."

"After what I have seen here, how not? It is good to touch the stone and pray the words of thanks." Miriam shut her eyes, lifted her hands, and spoke a soft refrain in Hebrew. Alathea responded with a soft *amen*, accented such that Amanda did not at first realize what she had just heard.

The curtains did not jerk back this time. Instead they were drawn back slowly, revealing an older gentleman, accompanied by a nurse and Dr. Korban. The senior doctor translated, "I call out to the Lord, and he answers me from his holy mountain. From the Lord comes deliverance." He gave Amanda a kindly glance. "You recognize these words, perhaps?"

"They are verses in the third Psalm."

He glanced back at Dr. Korban, then said, "And so a nurse who is no longer a nurse comes to Israel on holiday. This is true?"

"Yes."

"And how does a tourist from America come to be in Bet Jola? It is not, as you see, a destination for many tourists."

"Miriam asked me to come. We met at the Wailing Wall. I went there to pray, and Miriam asked me to put a prayer in the stones for her. About Rochele."

The three Israelis mirrored astonishment. They spoke with Miriam in Hebrew, who shrugged and nodded at the same time. Her tone was matter-of-fact, as was the soft embrace she gave to mother and daughter together. The elder doctor and the nurse and Dr. Korban all watched in silence as Miriam started off, leaning on her cane. The doctor asked her something, to which the old woman gave another abrupt wave. The doctor turned and spoke to the nurse, who hurried out. He said to Amanda, "We will arrange for a car to take her home."

"Thank you. The walk over was a lot for her."

"All right, madame. To the business of healing. It has been years since we treated a case of G-6PD. Even here in the Middle East it is very rare. So tell us how you would treat this."

"The enzyme test, obviously. And . . ."

"Yes? Please speak freely, madame. We are all in accord here. We have cared for Rochele her entire life. I was on duty the night she arrived. Before that I treated her father, and was there with the family to say *kaddish*. So tell us."

Amanda had made careful study of the data available on the illness, most of which had to be translated. "The patients with acute symptoms like Rochele follow a fairly steady pattern of improvement and decline. This is tied to the level of healthy blood cells. How long has it been since her last fever?"

Korban returned to the file on the treatment table. "Forty-two days."

"Which tallies with the jaundiced complexion. She is weakening again. Anything could set her off, probably an allergic reaction, since she's so well cared for. We need to strengthen her immediately."

"How is this done?"

"A blood transfusion today, followed by regular dialysis. Once a month should do it. When her strength starts to build by not suffering from regular fevers, you can cut back to once every three months."

He spoke at length with Alathea, who continued to glance at Amanda with something akin to awe. That done, he asked, "Anything more?"

"You need to hold Rochele to a strict diet, building up her weight and strength. Stop keeping her indoors. She needs to begin adjusting to normal life, and that includes accepting the occasional allergy. After six months she needs to be tested for what analgesics she can accept, because there will be fevers, and she will need to be given something to help stabilize the symptoms. Aspirin is usually better for the patient than paracetamol. There are others, more expensive, but still . . ."

Korban said, "We are speaking of an end of treatments that have filled this file. We are speaking of a child brought to life. What is the cost of a few pills?"

"No dried beans of any kind, and no hummus," Amanda went on. "And no sulfas. Not ever. When I get back to Florida, I can e-mail you my research dossier."

"Florida, how nice. My grandchildren all beg for a trip to Disney World." He spoke to Alathea, then to Korban, who replied in English, "It will be done."

"And now, good woman, we should let you go back to seeing our country."

Amanda exchanged farewells with Alathea. The mother's words needed no translation. Rochele gifted her with a tiny embrace. Amanda traced a finger along the child's face, shared another smile with her mother, then allowed the younger doctor to usher her outside. As they passed through the clinic's waiting area, the nurse she had seen inside was standing by the reception desk, surrounded by a half dozen other staffers. They all turned and stared as Amanda passed. She smiled a farewell and said to Dr. Korban, "You have a good staff here."

He pretended to shrug it off, but Amanda knew he was pleased. "I must apologize for my attitude."

"You are a good doctor. You have done your best by Rochele. If I had been in your position, I would have acted much worse."

"Not for an instant do I believe that." He waved to one of the men standing in the alley's shade. "We have cars for the infirm who must come for treatment. The least we can do is offer you a ride back to your hotel."

"Thank you." Amanda had a sudden thought. That first morning when she was trying to find which bus to take, the hotel receptionist had said this village was close to Bethlehem. She asked, "How far is Bethlehem from here?"

"Fifteen kilometers. You wish to go there?"

The desire rose up like a hunger. She had given up the chance to travel there with the tour group when she and Emily had struck out on their own. And tomorrow was her last day. This was her only chance. "Please."

"The hospital drivers cannot go through the checkpoints. These are official cars leased by the health department. You will have to take a taxi or walk into town. But he can wait and take you back to Jerusalem when you are done." He waved off her protests. "For the tourist lady who has brought back our child from the grave, what is such a thing? Nothing, that is what."

Amanda waited while he talked with the driver, then said, "I can't thank you enough."

"For what do you thank me? This I am not understanding."

"Last year I suffered a personal tragedy. I stopped working as a nurse. Now . . . I don't know what is going to happen when I get home. But I know the child in there is not the only one who has been healed."

"Madame, it gives me great peace to know we have given something in return for your gift to us." Dr. Korban bowed over her hand. "I urge you to go help the other little ones in your country, those who cry out in need."

CHAPTER TWENTY-ONE

The Judean hills above the road Amanda traveled gleamed in the afternoon light. The rocky scrubland had turned to molten gold. The fields of ancient olive trees were burnished with a timeless splendor. Amanda rolled down her window and let the hot desert wind rush over her. The driver smiled at her pleasure and turned on the radio. A woman sang in a tongue she did not understand, spicing the world with more mystery.

As Amanda stood in line at the checkpoint, she talked with a couple from Michigan. When they heard she was on her own, they insisted she join them for the trip into town. Amanda thanked them from the heart, relieved not to be entering this strange town alone.

The tour bus took them through the sprawling outer city. Amanda could see that many of the others were disappointed by what they saw. But for her it was very similar to Bet Jola, just another impoverished town struggling to make ends meet.

The tour guide spoke through the loudspeaker, explaining that because they were coming in the afternoon during the Christmas season, the parking lot closest to the Church of the Nativity was already full. They were going to be relegated to a parking area beyond the central market. They would arrange a taxi for anyone who could not walk the half mile.

Amanda loved the market. It was a vibrant tumult, filled with every imaginable sort of person and dress, from Western fashion to dark-robed women who saw the world through tight eye slits. The market sold everything from clothes to meat to refrigerators to parrots. The air was thick with spices and over-ripe fruit and truck fumes. Birds squawked and radios blared.

And so it was that she arrived at Manger Square that fronted the church. Amanda wiped the sweat from her face and found herself humming. Helping to heal the little one had left her almost giddy with joy. She hoped that there was something in the experience that would last beyond this first moment, that there would be something she could take back with her to Florida, and home, and the hospital, and Chris.

Her companions from the bus were very kind. As they waited in the line that snaked across the baking stones of the plaza, they introduced themselves and talked about where they had been. Amanda let the words wash over her, enjoying their company but not feeling the need to respond with more than a smile and the occasional nod. The market and the plaza were filled with hawkers and children begging for coins. The tour guide employed a very sharp tongue to protect her charges. Amanda felt as though the afternoon was making a special effort to shield her.

They waited almost an hour before they were permitted

through the tiny Door of Humility, a portal that forced even children to bend over to enter. Inside the ancient basilica the guide raised her voice to be heard over the babble of hundreds and hundreds of other visitors. The church's age was hotly disputed, but it was certain that at least some of the chamber where they now stood was set in place within three centuries of the Savior's death. Most of the others in her adopted group strained to hear above the clamor. Amanda remained on the fringe of the group.

They joined another line, this one leading to the Grotto of the Nativity. The chamber at the base of the narrow stone stairs was cool and much quieter, though the crowd was very dense. A silver star planted in the chamber floor marked the point where Jesus had been born. Amanda watched many of the others move forward to touch the star or kneel and pray at its edge. She allowed the throng to press her back against the side wall, where she found herself standing next to another of their group, an elderly gentleman who read from a pocket-sized New Testament. He noticed her gaze, smiled, and shifted the book over to where she could read with him.

Amanda read the words from Luke: *Greetings, you who are highly favored! The Lord is with you.*

The grotto was ancient in a manner that Amanda had never imagined might truly exist. The ceiling lamps held electric bulbs now, but they were encased in hand-blown glass, and the oil wicks were still visible. The walls were lined with paintings called icons, all of which were over a thousand years old.

Do not be afraid, Mary, you have found favor with God. You will conceive and give birth to a son, and you are to call him

Jesus. He will be great and will be called the Son of the Most High.

The chamber was suddenly filled with song. A group from Italy sang a chorale in four-part harmony. The music rang through the chamber, a chant of resounding glory.

The Holy Spirit will come on you, and the power of the Most High will overshadow you. So the holy one to be born will be called the Son of God.

Amanda felt an overwhelming sense of power flow through her. An awakening that sent shivers through her frame, tiny quakes that grew in force until she felt as though she vibrated like a human tuning fork. The words on the page seemed illuminated with a holy fire.

Amanda found herself there in the grotto with Mary. Hearing not the angel, but the young woman's fears. How tempted she must have been to give into them! The prospect of giving birth to the Holy One, balanced against all the woes of this world and all the pressures of life and tradition. And yet she found the strength not just to respond, but to *continue*. Amanda lifted her gaze to the polished stones of the grotto's ceiling. The glory and the agony. Was this not the way of all mothers? The hope and the terrible anxieties?

The perfection of the heavenly gift was balanced against the tremendous burdens of motherhood. It was true for every mother. Emily and Frank with the child they lost, not to mention the crisis they endured with Lucy. Alathea and her two years of sleepless worry over little Rochele. All the little ones

Amanda had cared for in the hospital, all the mothers who had sat by the crisis cribs and wept and prayed and begged for their babies to live, to grow, to thrive.

That was why she had not been able to enter the ward that day, Amanda realized. She could not face her own pain, much less the distress of other terrified mothers. She no longer possessed the distance and the balance required to comfort the ones who were brought into her care.

But was it truly gone? Had she not handled herself well with Rochele? Could she not at least try and return to the hospital, and confront her past and her present fears?

And what of Chris? *That* was the question she had not yet faced. Because it was not just about loving her husband with a full and giving and joyful heart. It had *never* been about that.

To give Chris what he wanted, she had to face her greatest fear of all.

She had to accept the risk of becoming pregnant again.

She had to *want* this.

But how was this possible? How could she give herself to any such impossible quest? How could she put aside her fears and her awareness of the bleak dark pit that loomed nine months beyond that moment?

The song ended, and in the echoing silence that followed, Amanda heard the words as clearly as if they had been spoken directly into her ear. Straight to her heart.

Because she was not alone.

Because the healing and the strength were already hers.

The same gift that the angel had offered to Mary was given to her as well. Freely and unconditionally. The strength to face tomorrow.

Amanda whispered the words on the page she could not read through her liquid veil, the words that echoed down two thousand years, from mother to mother. "I am the Lord's servant. May it be to me according to your word."

CHAPTER TWENTY-TWO

C hris puttered around the house until it was time to
leave for the airport and meet Emily's flight. While
he watered the hydrangeas, he had a long meander-
ing phone conversation with Kent Avery. They discussed who
should be promoted into Chris's current job. They discussed
meeting with the outside auditors the following week. Chris listened carefully but heard no suggestion of regret from Kent over
his decision.

He weeded the flower bed and trimmed the hedges at the
back of their yard. He painted one of the gutters and replaced a
couple of lights. He cleaned the kitchen counter and vacuumed
the living room carpet. He had always liked spending his down-
time doing small chores. It reminded him of growing up, when
he and all his siblings were expected to pitch in around the house.
When it was time, Chris showered and dressed. He started down
the hall, when his footsteps were slowed by a sudden desire to
enter the forbidden zone.

There had never been any discussion about what to do with the room at the back of the house. The door was only opened by the cleaner who came once a week. Chris retraced his steps, passed their bedroom, and reached for the door. The knob felt cold to the touch. He opened the door and stepped inside.

He and Amanda had painted the room blue, as pale and clear as the Florida sky at dawn. The two windows were sheltered by palms lining the side of their backyard. The room smelled vaguely of disinfectant. Chris walked over and ran one finger along the crib's frame. The tall table for changing the baby was polished and as bare as the walls. Chris stood in the center of the room and did a slow circle. He felt slightly hollow, a faint whisper of regret. But otherwise it was just a room. As he shut the door behind him, he decided his visit had been necessary to moving on.

If only Amanda could feel the same.

～◌～

Chris was locking his front door, on his way to the airport to meet Emily, when he decided it was time to phone his sister and say for certain that they would not be coming for Christmas. He went back inside and seated himself at the dining room table. Chris knew Amanda would go if he asked. Especially now, after what sounded like such an important personal time in Israel. And sitting there at the table he realized just how much he personally wanted to go. He loved his family and he reveled in these gatherings. But this needed to be done.

He took a long breath and dialed his sister's number.

"Well, *finally*." Claire's hands were busy; he could hear her clattering about some dishes as she greeted him. *"Please* tell me you've phoned to say you're coming."

Chris could hear the kids in the background and felt a sudden pang over missing the chance to watch them explode into their presents on Christmas morning. He could almost smell the roasting turkey. Claire made a traditional stuffing, starting with chestnuts she ground herself and smoked Virginia sausage. "I'm sorry, Claire. I want to. But it just isn't possible."

She was silent a long moment. Chris dreaded the eruption, the anger with which Claire responded to everything that encroached on family time. Instead all she said was, "Here I was worried you might be delayed because of the snowstorm. They're predicting a blizzard."

Her soft disappointment caught him unaware. He hated causing her such sadness. "Claire, I need to do what's best for my wife. And she needs to be here. In our home."

"Isn't she off traveling somewhere?"

"Yes, she is. As a matter of fact, I'm driving to the Orlando airport as soon as I get off the phone. The friend she traveled with is returning early from Israel. Her husband has gone into the hospital. He had an emergency hip replacement."

"Isn't Amanda coming back with her?"

"No, she's staying for the remaining two days. Like they'd planned."

"Your wife is across the ocean in a foreign country and she's *alone?"*

"That's right."

"Aren't you *worried?"*

"Not at all." Chris thought back over their most recent conversations and added, "Matter of fact, I'm proud of her."

"What could possibly be so important that she would want to stay longer?"

"She is healing."

"Can't she come up here and heal too?" A trace of her normal heat rose in her voice. "Explain to me why your wife can travel to *Israel* but can't come up to have *Christmas* with *family!*"

Chris had to stop and swallow hard. "Amanda has a gift. She lost it when she lost our baby. Since she's been gone, I've had a chance to see her as she was, and see us in that same light. And now I know her making this journey was important to us both. For the first time since last year she's looking beyond her loss and healing. Now she needs to come home, have some space, and cement these lessons into her life here."

Claire was slow in responding. "You sound different."

"I only know I want to be," Chris replied. "For Amanda."

"I'll miss you, little brother. We all will."

"Likewise. Pray for us, will you?"

"For your information, I've never *stopped* praying."

He grinned into the sunlight. "Thanks, Claire."

"You're welcome." Another pause, then, "What is this gift of Amanda's?"

"She carries other people's burdens." Chris felt his throat turn raw by the effort it took to fight the words through the sudden lump. "She makes them her own."

∾

His phone rang just as he was passing their church and approaching the causeway bridge. He assumed it was Claire calling back. "This is Chris."

Instead, the lawyer representing Campaeo said, "Evan Crouch here, Mr. Vance. Your secretary was kind enough to give me your cell phone number."

"Just a moment, please." Chris could feel his body clenching as though preparing for an incoming blow. He pulled into the church parking lot and cut the motor. He sent up a quick prayer, a silent plea that he would find the strength not to lose the joy that filled his heart. Then he took a long breath and said, "What can I do for you?"

"I was wondering if you might come by our office."

"Do we have an agreement on terms?" When the lawyer hesitated, Chris went on, "Yes or no, Mr. Crouch. Because if your clients have accepted our requirements, then I would be happy to meet. But not until then."

"Give me a moment, please."

While he waited, Chris stared out the front windshield. The inland waterway sparkled beyond the palms rimming the lot. He felt a vivid sense of satisfaction, as though he had taken a tremendously important step. He could not control the other person's attitude. He could not declare what would happen to his company. All he could do was his best. And part of his best was asking God for help.

The lawyer came back with, "Where are you now, Mr. Vance?"

"On my way to the Orlando airport."

"Can you give us fifteen minutes?"

"My friend is coming back from Israel for a family emergency. I can't be late. Besides, I don't see—"

"We'll meet you there. Do you know the Hyatt inside the airport? There's a restaurant to the right of the reception area. We'll be at a table by the window."

◦◦◦

Despite its location in the main airport terminal, the Orlando Hyatt possessed a molded elegance. The hotel rose like a four-sided sculpture above the west departure gates. The hotel's lobby was tucked discretely away, directly over the largest security checkpoint in Florida. Chris entered the hotel lounge and marveled anew at how silent the place was. No walls separated this space from the constant din below. Yet the only sound that pierced the natural buffers was a child's cry, there and gone.

He headed down the long hall connecting to the convention rooms and the restaurant, gave his name to the hostess, and was ushered to a table overlooking the runways. The three men and one young woman rose to their feet at his approach. But this meeting was all about a rotund brawler with a lion's mane of gray hair. Chris knew this was Jorge Coelho, owner of Campaeo, because he had researched the man carefully. Coelho was known as a man who loved a good fight almost as much as he did fine food and beautiful women. He personified the Latin way of life, living large and taking pleasure in almost everything he did, including the crushing of all opponents.

"But this cannot be!" the man boomed. "Chris Vance is a dragon! He breathes fire and walks away unsinged! He is not this young athlete who stands before me!"

"Mr. Coelho." From another supplier Chris had learned the man liked to use his bone-crushing grip to force an advantage. So he rammed his own hand in overly fast, a tactic that had been shown to him by a friend and self-defense fanatic. Chris set his thumb and forefinger on the hand's pressure points and clenched with all his might.

The man's eyes widened in surprise. Chris then broke off the grip, sweeping his hand down and away. Showing with grim determination that he was not to be controlled. Or handled. Or intimidated.

Coelho smiled thinly. "You must tell me, Mr. Vance. Is it necessary for us to speak as adversaries?"

"Not at all. It is totally your choice."

"Good. That is very good indeed. Because in my country, life is to be lived at all times. In every hour of every day. Pleasure is a flower to be plucked and smelled and enjoyed. Including in the work. To live and dance and sing. With friends, yes, friends! That is the Brazilian way."

Chris was tempted to ask if it was also the Brazilian way to cheat and lie and swindle. But he decided that could wait. He remained silent.

Jorge Coelho must have seen something of the unspoken, for his demeanor changed. A tight, hard gleam surfaced in those dark eyes. But his smile remained in place. "Shall I start with a question, I wonder? Yes, why not. Tell me, Chris. May I call you Chris? Excellent. And I am Jorge. Tell me. How can a man succeed in business if he does not test the boundaries? How else can he learn how far he can go, how high his profits?"

Chris did not need to think that one over. "By building trust. By creating an ethical business structure. By seeking to grow in a way that gives profit and hope to everyone involved."

"Sit, sit, please. Will you take coffee? Here, let me pour you a cup. Sugar and cream? It is most interesting, what you say. But tell me this. Whose company is succeeding, and whose is faced with bankruptcy?"

Chris found himself genuinely liking this man. It was

ridiculous, he knew. Jorge Coelho was an international charmer, an elegant destroyer of companies and dreams. Chris might as well climb in the cage with a hungry leopard. But the Brazilian was also cheerful and exuberant. His energy infected everyone around him.

Chris replied, "The concept is not mine. It has guided American companies for five generations. Henry Ford paid his employees enough that they could buy the cars they made, and thus fueled the nation's growth. My company's aim has been to treat all our employees and customers and suppliers with the same level of honesty and fairness. Hopefully Avery Electronics will weather this economic crisis. But regardless of my company's future, the principles of ethical business will remain."

"And how, pray tell, can you speak these words with such certainty? Perhaps the time for your business model is over, and the Campaeo method is the future."

Chris smiled. "Worlds may pass away. But these principles will remain."

"And you know this how?"

"Because they are grounded in the eternal."

The fierce metallic glint descended from his gaze to his smile. "I want you to come work for me."

"I . . . what?"

"Executive vice president of the new Melbourne plant. My company's name, Campaeo, you know what this means?"

"Champion."

"Yes. Exactly." He prodded Chris with a stubby forefinger. "Come and work for a champion. That is my offer."

"Thank you, I . . ." Chris forced himself to his feet. "I will consider . . ."

"Sit, please. I dislike looking up at people."

"My friend's flight is due in soon."

"My assistant can see to this." He motioned to the young lady seated at the table's far end, who rose instantly to her feet. "What is your friend's name?"

"Emily Wright." His voice sounded faint to his own ears. "She's coming from Israel, but this flight started in London."

"Lovely country, Israel. We do much good business there." He smiled away the young staffer. "Now then. Please do sit and tell me what you think of my invitation."

Chris knew he was being offered a huge opportunity. A chance to walk away from a failing company and start a new life with a successful one. But all he could think to say was, "My good name is all I have."

"Yes? I'm sorry, this means precisely what?"

Chris licked his dry lips. He reached out and took the cup of coffee. He was glad to see his hand did not shake. "In order to work for you, I would require complete financial independence. The subsidiary pays all its bills on time. It honors all contracts as they are written. I meet the letter of all obligations. I have total control of hiring, firing, subcontractors, and quality."

Jorge's gaze tightened. He drummed his fingers on the table. Across from him, the attorney made rapid notes. "And your terms?"

"I'm sorry, I don't understand."

"Come, come, Chris. We are adults here. Your terms. What you want. For yourself."

"What difference does that make? We're not even talking the same language."

Jorge's jovial mask slipped away, and the hungry predator

was revealed. "Your company faces ruin. You know this as well as I do. I am throwing you a lifeline. Perhaps the only one you will receive in these difficult times. I ask you for your terms."

Chris had to jack himself to his feet by pressing hard on the table. "I have just told you."

⌒

Chris rode the escalator down into the terminal's chaotic din. From the calm façade of the hotel and its elegant chambers to the reality of an airport and families and stress and life. He reached the bottom and realized he had no idea where to go. He searched the massive arrivals board but could not make heads or tails of the words. The flights and times might as well have been written in Sanskrit. He could not bear the thought of meeting Emily. He had to sit down. Just for a moment. Put some space between what had just happened and whatever came next.

He walked over and seated himself on an empty bench by the central fountain. The noise of children in the security lines rose up behind him. His life was just like this, chaotic and messy and filled with a thousand different voices, all clamoring for his attention. And Monday he was to begin his new job. President of a company that could very well soon fail.

He was so tempted to ride the escalator back up and accept the Brazilian's offer. The sense of isolation and fear was almost overwhelming. Chris pretended to rub his eyes. And he prayed. Or tried to. Though the words were as clogged in his brain as they had been upstairs on his tongue. He asked for some sign that he had done the right thing. And for the strength to get through the coming days. *Please.*

"Mr. Vance?"

He dropped his hand and turned around. He knew he should recognize the young woman. But just then he could not place her.

"Jane Sayer. I work with Campaeo's new US division. Mr. Campaeo sent me to meet your friend."

"Of course. I'm sorry . . ."

"Her flight has been delayed, she won't get in for another forty-five minutes." She hesitated, then added in a rush, "Sir, I just wanted to say, well, thank you."

"You . . . What?"

The young executive was probably in her late twenties. She had a runner's tight frame, balanced against deep plum-colored circles under her eyes. She wore a typical dark suit with a bolero tie and a silver brooch on her lapel that matched the tie-clasp. She was poised and intelligent and attractive. And, Chris suddenly realized, she was very close to the edge.

"I was responsible for researching you. I did it like I do a hundred other assignments. I was thorough and I was discreet. And I was crushed by what I learned."

The fountain's constant rush created a baffle that kept her words from escaping to the people flowing all around them. But there was nothing that could be done about the way she struggled for control, or hid the occasional tear, or the way she struggled against whatever was pressing up inside. People kept glancing their way, first to her, then to Chris, clearly wondering what he had done to upset her so badly.

Chris asked, "Would you like to sit down?"

She only managed to find the bench because he took hold of her arm and guided her down. "You are everything I was raised to be. And I want to ask you how you did it. How you maintained your standards. How you didn't give in."

Chris slid back to the bench's far edge so as to see her clearly. "You're from a believing family?"

"My father is a pastor."

"Where were you raised?"

"St. Louis until I was ten. Then he accepted a pulpit in Kansas City."

"Did you rebel against your faith?"

"No. Yes. I don't . . ." She swiped at her face, an impatient gesture. "I never really gave it much thought. I just assumed I could, you know, make it on my own."

"You're strong, you're intelligent, you're independent, you have a lot going for you."

"And every step I took seems to be the wrong one." She stared at the fountain, and Chris had a sudden impression that she let the fountain cry for her. "My life is such a mess. I've become a pro at ignoring just how unhappy I am. And then I started asking about you. I assumed it was a joke at first. That's how I treated it. A joke. And then I learned about your work with the church. Your stable family. Your community service with the group out of Kissimmee. Everywhere I asked, I heard people talk about how *good* you were." She struggled to open her purse and extracted a tissue. "And the way you handled yourself upstairs. I could just hear my father tell me this is what a man of faith can be inside the business world. This is what I walked away from."

Chris waited long enough to be certain she was finished, then replied, "It's never too late."

"I wouldn't even know where to start, unraveling all the mistakes."

"I can tell you that much." For the first time since he arrived, he felt light. Freed from his burdens. Because he knew with all his heart that his stumbling plea had been heard. And answered. "Would you like to pray with me?"

CHAPTER TWENTY-THREE

Nechama's family was incredibly kind and the dinner superb. They started with a variety of fresh Mediterranean delicacies, a salad of chopped coriander and mint, stuffed vine leaves, grilled peppers and eggplant drizzled in oil, on and on the dishes came. Afterward there was roast lamb spiced in a manner that left Amanda feeling as though she had been transported back to some ancient world. When she said as much, Nechama's husband nodded approval while his wife deposited yet more food upon her plate.

Nechama was, in fact, married to one of the attorneys she had mentioned, and another was her eldest son. Both men were tall and slender, with scraggly beards and skullcaps and starched white shirts and black pants and lace-up shoes. Nechama chided them constantly through the meal, filling their plates and waving the serving spoon like she was scolding two children. There was another son who lived in Tel Aviv and visited far too rarely, the one point Nechama and her husband agreed upon. Their daughter was married to a biochemist who was completing his doctorate in London. The son at dinner had a wife and three children, but they were off on a seaside holiday with the wife's parents. Which was why the son was here, he explained, winking at Amanda, being talked to like he was still nine years old.

The apartment was on a hilltop looking back toward the Old City and the Jaffa Gate. They took coffee on the terrace, where they insisted that Amanda recount the entire experience with Rochele, starting with the Wailing Wall and ending with the hospital doctor bowing over her hand.

When Amanda had thanked them and said her farewells, Nechama saw her downstairs. "Your flight home is when?"

"Tomorrow evening at nine."

"My son has business in Tel Aviv. He will drive you to the airport."

Amanda's protests went nowhere, so she accepted the inevitable with, "I can't thank you enough."

"You have heard the expression, next year in Jerusalem? So. Next year you will return. With your husband. I forget, his name again is what?"

"Chris. Christopher."

"You and Christopher. You come and stay with us. My husband agrees."

Amanda gaped. "We wouldn't want to be any trouble."

"What is trouble? The children are gone. We have too many empty rooms. Your husband, he is as nice as you?"

"Chris is wonderful," she replied, missing him intensely.

"Then it is settled." She embraced Amanda, her grip as fierce and impatient as the rest of her. "So. Next year in Jerusalem. You will not forget."

~◦·

After breakfast, Amanda walked through the grand plaza fronting the Jaffa Gate and selected a street at random. Stallholders
called to her and children followed and chattered. All around
her, tourists walked in tired clumps, sweltering in the desert
heat. The stones already shimmered in the morning sunlight,
and shadows from the high walls cut jagged edges across her
path. The heat was very different from Florida, free as it was of
humidity and compressed with all the odors of a cramped and
vibrant city. Soon enough she left the crowds behind. The people
of Jerusalem's old town glanced at her, then away. Unless they
were selling something, theirs was a closed world, segmented
by history and conflict and what she could only imagine was a
hard life.

She entered a plaza filled with food stalls and bought a cup
of pomegranate juice. She took a seat in the sunlight and fingered the two slips of paper in her pocket, the prayer from Chris
and another she had written out that morning. Her own prayer
was a repetition of Mary's words. *I am the Lord's servant. May it
be according to your word.* She had no idea whether she possessed
the strength to actually deal with whatever was to come next.
But Mary's example was something she wanted to carry back
with her.

Miriam was there waiting for her on the bench outside the
Wall's barriers, and they greeted each other warmly. As they
passed through the security checkpoint and started down the
hall leading to the women's section, Amanda was filled with a
sudden restless hunger. She positively ached to hold Chris again.
And yet even stronger than the longing she felt for her husband

was the desire to hold fast to the miracles she had experienced since her arrival.

Amanda helped Miriam seat herself on a bench facing the Wall. The old woman shifted her cane to the other arm and reached into her voluminous purse. She took her time drawing out a pen and piece of paper. "Tell me how I can pray for you."

Amanda lowered herself down to the stone seat. "Excuse me?"

"There is little an old woman in a poor village can do for a stranger visiting from America," Miriam told her. "But this I can offer. *Nu.* So give me the words you would like me to offer up each day."

Amanda hesitated, then confessed, "I want to take back with me all that I have learned here in your land."

"Your heart is good, child. I am honored by your words. And God, he is pleased." She bent over the paper, writing with painful and determined effort. Then she rolled up the paper like a tiny scroll and handed it over. "Go and add my prayers with your own."

CHAPTER TWENTY-FOUR

Emily was so quiet during the journey from the airport, Chris assumed she had dozed off. But as he took the Melbourne exit from I-95, she asked, "Do you want to tell me what's troubling you?"

"I'm not even sure how to put it all into words."

She hesitated, then asked, "Is it Frank?"

"Not at all. Don't think about that for an instant." It was his turn to pause and collect himself. "Actually, it's work. And I'd rather not talk about it because I haven't told Amanda yet."

"All right." She rubbed her face. "Do you mind if we stop by the hospital on our way?"

"Of course not."

"I don't mind having to come home early. I wish I had been home when he fell. But it sounds like everything went as well as it possibly could have."

"It did, and he's fine."

"I can't thank you enough for taking care of him like you did."

"I enjoyed doing it."

"With everything you've had going on, it must have been a strain."

"It's been good to have something that pulls me out of myself. I know that sounds crazy but it's true."

She studied the sunlight and the road and the palms. "I'm afraid of losing it, Chris."

"I'm sorry, what?"

"The feeling I had in Israel. The sense of God's closeness. The answer to prayers. I want to bring the miracle home with me." She looked over. "Now who sounds crazy."

Chris pulled into the hospital's parking garage, found a space, and cut the motor, taking his time. "How is Amanda?"

"Exactly like you've heard." Emily reached for the door handle. "I suspect she is hoping for the same thing I am."

Chris moved beside her, their footsteps echoing through the concrete chamber. "I'm glad you asked her to go."

"Not nearly as glad as I am. We left for Israel as good neighbors. We're returning as best friends."

In the elevator Chris started to explain that Frank had been moved to the sixth floor, which was great news, because it was the ward for people well on their way to full healing. And that he'd spoken the day before with Frank's physical therapist, a no-nonsense woman with the manner of a polite drill sergeant, and she'd said that Frank was making enormous progress for a man of any age, much less one of his years. But as Chris started to speak, he saw that Emily's eyes were clenched shut and her shoulders were hunched, and he realized that the woman was praying. He hesitated, then placed his hand on her shoulder.

Then the doors opened and he led Emily down the hall to

Frank's room. Emily froze in the doorway and started weeping at the sight of their pregnant daughter seated beside her husband's bed, the two of them holding hands.

Chris walked away, glad for such a wonderful reason to smile. And to hope.

CHAPTER TWENTY-FIVE

The flight left on time and flew west into the night. Amanda slept most of the way to London and woke with the dawn. She walked the endless hallway to the Heathrow Airport transfer desk, took the bus to Terminal Three, and located her departure gate. She bought a coffee and phoned Chris. Amanda knew he was holding something back. She suspected it was more bad news about his company and ached for them both. He deserved better.

It all came back to that.

She boarded the plane for Orlando and settled into another airplane seat. She ate another airplane meal, then tried to watch an in-flight movie and found it only made her eyes hurt. She shut off the screen and thought about what awaited her upon arrival. She wanted to return home and give to Chris the comfort and the love and the joy he deserved. Whatever happened in the world beyond their door, she wanted him to know that she waited for him with open heart and arms. That she was there to give him everything she was, everything she had, everything God had entrusted to her.

And she wanted to return to nursing. The decision came to her full blown. She wanted to be there for the next little Rochele who arrived with her own desperate need. Amanda knew there were any number of nurses as well qualified as herself. If she had anything special to give it was her ability to love and cherish and pray. She wanted this. What was more, she was *ready*.

Amanda walked down the aisle and asked the hostess for a glass of water. As she drank, her eyes fell upon a newspaper tucked into the magazine rack. She had not read a paper since leaving Florida. She pulled it out and scanned the headlines. When her gaze fell upon one story, suddenly she was no longer sleepy.

The headline read *First Storm of Season Wreaks Havoc Along Eastern Seaboard*. There was a photograph of the Washington airport blanketed in snow, with a plane slipped off the runway and trapped in a gully. Amanda read how the early snowstorm had blanketed Washington, DC, Virginia, and the Carolinas that very morning. And how another was due to strike in six days, threatening to disrupt the holidays.

This meant they couldn't travel to Virginia for Christmas. Chris surely wanted to go, yet she knew he would be willing to do whatever she wanted. All she needed was a reason not to go, and here it was, in full-color display. But Amanda felt no relief over being spared the prospect of a massive family gathering. Which was very odd, since if she had been asked about it before traveling to Israel, she would have said a chance to avoid the memories of what had happened the previous year was a genuine Christmas gift. Instead, she felt as though she was missing something important.

She fell asleep again, still mulling over what could possibly be the benefit of fighting their way north for a holiday on ice.

This time Amanda knew where she was, flying at forty thousand feet, the muffled roar of the engines filling the space beyond her closed eyelids. She drifted away, then back, each time returning to the same vague hope. That she would return with the lessons gained, her healing intact.

The journey and the jet lag gave her a sense of disembodiment, as though she was tied to the world by the lightest of strings. She slept and she dreamed, and was aware that she was dreaming. She saw herself rise from a cool stone bench. She crossed a floor of close-cut stone, and now instead of the engine's sibilant rush she heard the chorus of many women's voices, all rising together in a soft union of prayer and psalms. Amanda watched herself fit the prayer into the crack in the stone, one slip of paper among hundreds, thousands. She rested her fingers on the cool, dry surface.

Then she opened her eyes.

The light beyond the window was brilliant. Amanda leaned over and studied the scene below. There was not a cloud in the sky. They flew over a burnished snowscape. The world was flat and white and frozen. She studied the scene for a very long while, then leaned back and closed her eyes once more. But she did not sleep. She planned.

Amanda knew exactly what she needed to do.

⌒

Chris put as much of himself as he possibly could into that first embrace. He had not missed Amanda nearly so much that entire week as he did in this first instant of seeing her. He felt surrounded not only by her arms but also by the simple goodness of her. He could smell the vague odor of the long flight in her hair. He tasted the dryness of her lips. And as he looked into her eyes and saw the love, the calm acceptance of who he was, he knew he had no choice but to tell her everything.

He apologized three times, or perhaps four, in the telling. His apologies were not over what he said. It was in having taken so long to open up. He would have said it again but Amanda told him to stop. He talked through the drive down the emerald-clad Beachline Expressway and onto the I-95 corridor. He talked them off the highway and down the main thoroughfare leading to the hospital.

He paused then, long enough to ask if she wanted to see Frank.

"I can't, not with the new administrator and everything I'll have waiting for me," she replied. "Frank will understand. Emily will make sure of that."

He used a stoplight as an opportunity to glance over. She looked so calm, so steady. "Emily says you've become good friends."

"We've shared miracles," Amanda said. "Now tell me the rest."

So he did. About the Brazilian and the news about the company and the offer. He was still talking as they pulled into the drive. Amanda made no move to get out. "Is that all?"

"Yes. Well, no," he decided, and told her about Jane Sayer, the young executive who had met with him by the fountain. He described how they had prayed together, and then how he had phoned Jackie, the pastor who had brought Frank and his daughter together.

"I'm proud of you," Amanda said.

"It was really nice, having that sense of affirmation," he agreed. "And then seeing Emily yesterday, I wish you could have been there. Frank and Emily and their daughter, all together in the hospital room. I've carried those images with me."

"How are things with Claire?"

"Why do you ask?"

"Is she worried about the weather?"

"Borderline frantic is the better way to describe it." Now that she had accepted that Chris was not coming, Claire was using him as a sounding board, someone she could turn to with all her worries. Chris had found himself looking forward to the talks and the way he felt connected to the holiday gathering he would miss. "Wouldn't you rather wait and talk about this after you've rested?"

"We can't wait. This has to be done now."

"What does?"

"I want to call and invite her down."

Chris needed a few moments to shape one word. "What?"

"Claire and all the family. Tell them to come have Christmas with us."

"Honey, do you have any idea . . . There are nineteen of them."

"Twenty-one, counting us. If they all come. Which I assume they will. So the kids can camp out on the patio. And Emily and Frank can put up others. They've got three spare bedrooms, or two, if Lucy decides to have Christmas with them."

"Don't you need to ask them first?"

"I phoned Emily from the terminal before I came out to meet you. Their other three children are doing Christmas with the in-laws. Emily was thrilled with the idea of filling up her home. Frank was over the moon. He says nothing would make him get well faster than a house full of laughter." Amanda smiled. "What do you think?"

"I think . . . It's great. Claire will be thrilled and worried and she'll want to take over your kitchen."

"Then let her."

Chris studied his wife. "Are you sure this is what you want?"

"Yes, Christopher. I'm sure." Then she was reaching out and over, the light there in her eyes, warm and soft and so full of love he could dive in and lose himself. "It's so good to be home."

CHAPTER TWENTY-SIX

Amanda stood on her front lawn and watched the Christmas Eve sunset unfold.

The border between their yard and their neighbor's to the west was fashioned from bougainvillea and palm trees. Bougainvillea were odd plants, both hearty and temperamental. They would grow in sandy soil a block off the ocean, and their leaves rarely showed burn from salt or wind. But unless they were fed regularly, they stubbornly refused to bloom. Chris fertilized them in the fall and the spring. The result was a crimson and violet wall over eight feet high. The palms stood like calm sentinels against this riot of color.

The afternoon shadows shielded her from view. Amanda watched children race from her front door to the Wrights, chattering happily with Lucy, who managed quite a clip despite her distended belly. Emily and Frank had opened their extra bedrooms to two of the visiting families. All nineteen of Amanda's guests were here, filling the cul de sac with laughter. Frank's roar rose from the backyard. There was an instant's silence, then half a dozen kids roared back. As far as they were concerned they had arrived in Florida and adopted a new granddad.

"Amanda?" Chris came around the side of the house. He smiled at the sight of her nestled in between the palms. "What are you doing over here?"

"I just needed a moment alone."

"Do you want me to leave?"

"No." She reached for one of his arms and pulled it close, arching her back in a catlike motion so he knew to draw around behind her. It was an action from their early days together, fashioning themselves together. They would stand like this and watch sunsets or feel the wind or just breathe in harmony. Like now. "Let's be alone together."

He nestled in closer still and breathed the scent of her hair. "This is nice."

"Mmmm."

"I loved doing this with you. Standing like this on the boardwalk and watching the sunset. I always felt like we were dancing to the symphony of colors."

"You never told me that."

"Didn't I?" He shifted slightly. "Why did you need a moment alone?"

"My kitchen's been taken over by four other women and one of your nephews. Who is determined to show me everything he's learned in culinary school."

"Not to mention all the kids."

"They're everywhere," she agreed. "They've turned the living room into an imaginary castle and they're taking turns rescuing someone from the dungeon and fighting over which one gets to be Shrek."

"And the rocker from our nursery is the donkey they all want to ride." He touched the point where her hair met the collar of her shirt. "I could send them all away."

"Oh, sure."

"Just pack them in their cars and send them down the road. And we can have a quiet few days all to ourselves."

"Don't you dare. I like them being here."

"Do you really?"

"Yes, Chris." She drew his arms more tightly around her middle. "Really."

"Oh, good. You had me worried there for a minute." He swayed slightly, as though they were dancing to the wind rustling the palm fronds overhead. "Did I hear you talking to somebody at the hospital?"

"The new director. Again." The hospital director had phoned her six times since her return. He seemed nice enough, but he was desperately trying to convince her to stay on as his assistant.

"Have you made up your mind?"

"Not yet." She hesitated, then added, "But I'm thinking I might agree. Just for a year. I really don't feel any pressure to get back to nursing. So long as it's there on the horizon."

"Dr. Henri would like that."

"Has he spoken to you?"

"We talked. But he's too polite to say anything outright. He just said what a great help you are."

They remained like that for a time, content in their silence. Amanda loved the strength of his arms and the feel of protection and love they offered. She was about to say that when a flock of children came screaming around the house, towels and snorkels and fins in their grasps. They yelled for the two of them to come and play in the pool. Chris motioned for her to stay where she was and headed them off. He let them grab hold of his hands and pull him protesting across the grass. Amanda watched him go, happy in the knowledge that she would have many times ahead to tell him what a good and loving man he was.

As she stood there thinking about all these things, a car pulled into the cul de sac and a young woman got out. She looked out of place; in a Christmas season of T-shirts and bathing suits and sandals, she wore a pearl-gray business suit. Where the street was filled with family and laughter, she stood alone and forlorn.

Amanda left her shelter and walked over. "Can I help you?"

The woman said, "I shouldn't be here."

"Have we met?"

"No. But I know you from your photograph. You're the wife of Chris Vance."

Amanda realized who she faced. "You're the lady from Campaeo. The one who researched my husband."

"He told you about me?"

"Yes, he did." Amanda smiled.

The young woman was very attractive, were it not for the hard edges and her struggle not to cry. "Can you tell me, did Mr. Vance . . . Has he accepted Campaeo's offer?"

"Not yet. He's praying about it. We both are."

"Will you tell him something for me?"

"Why don't you come tell him yourself? Though I have to warn you, it is total chaos inside. We're hosting his family for Christmas. We're twenty-one, counting Chris and myself."

Amanda held the young woman's hand and led her out of

the street. She had dealt with more than her share of such crisis situations. She knew how much a caring voice and a warm touch could mean. "Can I offer you something to drink?"

"I quit my job."

Amanda stopped because the woman did. "Is that what you need to tell Chris?"

"No. I wanted him to know that I gave my life to Jesus last night. The quitting was necessary after that."

Amanda felt as though her smile would split her face. "Chris will be thrilled. Truly. Now you really must—"

"Jorge Coelho lied to your husband."

"Excuse me?"

"Coelho has done everything he can to undermine your husband's company. And he's failed."

A clutch of shrieking children piled around the corner of the Wrights' home. Amanda drew the young lady over to the shelter of the bordering palms. "Why would he do such a thing?"

"Because that's how he operates. Campaeo is desperate for Avery's technology. There is no other company whose product even comes close. Jorge Coelho wants to buy them out."

"Kent Avery won't sell."

"Which is why he's tried so hard to force them. There was a client Avery went after last December."

Despite the warm sunset breeze, Amanda felt a sudden chill. "I remember. They went bankrupt . . . That was you?"

"They were in trouble. Campaeo used their influence in the market to push them over the edge." The woman turned away. "Tell your husband I'm sorry. But his company is going to make it. And Campaeo will agree to his terms."

The woman formed a lonely silhouette in the dusk. She

walked away with both arms clenched tightly around her middle, canted slightly to one side as though her ribs ached. Or her heart.

Amanda found herself running before she understood the reason why. She reached the young woman and asked, "What are your plans for dinner?"

"I . . ." She unwound her arms long enough to wipe her face. "What?"

"Why don't you join us?"

The woman's gesture took in the dusky emptiness of the road that awaited her. "But . . . it's Christmas."

Once more Amanda took her by the hand. "Exactly."

More from Davis Bunn

Visit **DavisBunn.com** for

- · Reading Group Guide for *Prayers of a Stranger*
- · Q&A with the Author
- · Davis's blog
- · A complete list of books by Davis Bunn

Connect with **Davis Bunn**

 Davis Bunn – author

@davisbunn

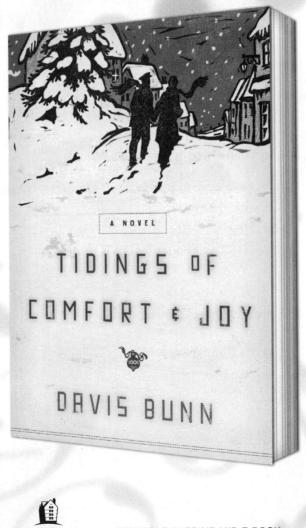

B RIAN THOUGHT HE HAD NO FUTURE. Now he has the chance to start over . . . if he can solve the mysteries of the past found inside Castle Keep.

H illsboro is a town where people are stubborn and fiercely protective of their own. But this winter will bring changes both welcome and unwelcome— and the town's greatest sorrow will become the source of its deepest healing.

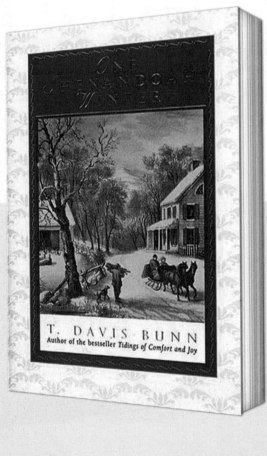

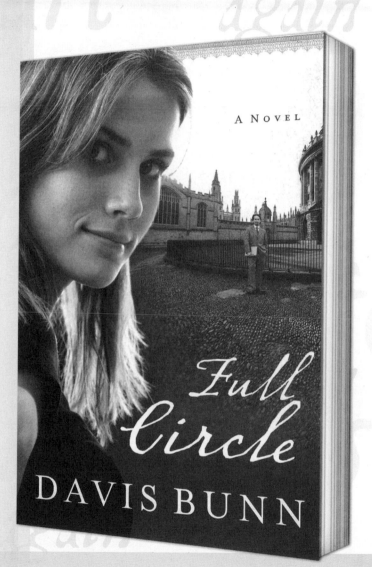

ABOUT THE AUTHOR

 *Davis Bunn* is an internationally acclaimed author who has sold more than seven million books in fifteen languages. He has been honored with three Christy Awards for excellence in historical and suspense fiction and is a sought-after lecturer in the art of writing. For over a decade, Bunn has served as writer in Residence at Regent's Park College, Oxford University, and was recently named Lecturer in the university's new creative writing program. Visit his website at davisbunn.com.